JUDE SAVES THE WORLD

RONNIE RILEY

Scholastic Press / New York

Library of Congress Cataloging-in-Publication Data

Names: Riley, Ronnie, author.

Title: Jude saves the world / Ronnie Riley.

Description: First edition. | New York : Scholastic Inc., 2023. | Audience:
Ages 8–12. | Audience: Grades 4–6. | Summary: Twelve-year-old Jude Winters
is dealing with ADHD while trying to figure out how to tell their old-fashioned
grandparents about their nonbinary status—but now they have another problem:
Stevie, a previously popular girl at school has been ostracized because she has
a crush on another girl, and Jude wants to help her cope as well.

Identifiers: LCCN 2022034005 (print) | LCCN 2022034006 (ebook) |
ISBN 9781338855876 (hardcover) | ISBN 9781338855890 (ebook)

Subjects: LCSH: Gender-nonconforming children—Juvenile fiction. | Attention-
deficit hyperactivity disorder—Juvenile fiction. | Lesbians—Juvenile fiction. |
Grandparents—Juvenile fiction. | Social acceptance—Juvenile fiction. | Identity
(Psychology)—Juvenile fiction. | Friendship—Juvenile fiction. | CYAC:
Gender-nonconforming people—Fiction | Attention-deficit hyperactivity disorder—
Fiction. | Lesbians—Fiction. | Grandparents—Fiction. | Social acceptance—Fiction. |
Identity—Fiction. | Friendship—Fiction. | BISAC: JUVENILE FICTION /
LGBTQ | JUVENILE FICTION / Family / Multigenerational

Classification: LCC PZ7.1.R556 Ju 2023 (print) | LCC PZ7.1.R556 (ebook) |
DDC 813.6 [Fic]—dc23/eng/20220815

LC record available at https://lccn.loc.gov/2022034005

LC ebook record available at https://lccn.loc.gov/2022034006

To my twelve-year-old self.
I'm sorry I didn't have the language to describe what I was feeling, but I do now, and you'd be proud of me.

And to Gus, Darcy, and Reggie,
for I would not still be here if these cats hadn't imprinted their paws on my soul during my darkest hours. I miss you.

Dear readers,

I know what it's like to worry about what may or may not be in a book, especially when it comes to queer and trans stories. I'm here to reassure you.

Jude Winters, the main character of this book, is nonbinary and uses they/them pronouns. While Jude and their friends experience different coming outs, all ends well. They also experience deadnaming and misgendering *off the page*, so you will never learn Jude's birth name or assigned gender. If these are new words to you, please reference the Queer Glossary at the back.

I hope you find unconditional love and safety in Jude's story.

With love,

Ronnie ♡

CHAPTER 1

Sometimes all you need is someone next to you to make everything okay. I've already found that person here in Aberdeen Falls, and I'm only twelve.

And right now I'm trying to be patient while my best friend, Dallas, finishes listening to his Song of the Day. I *do* already feel better being beside him, but it's not nearly enough. I pick at the hole on the back of the bus seat with my fingers.

I already know what he's going to say. It won't be like when Mom tells me the whole world doesn't rest on my shoulders. But heck, what if it does? What if I end up being the hero? And Dallas and I go on a huge quest to save the earth from mutant alien robots?

Anything seems better than doing the same thing over and over again—which is exactly what last night was. A repeat of the same Monday for the last two years: dinner with my grandparents who are from the Stone Age. They say and do hurtful things without even realizing it, and Mom always has to remind me that they aren't as open-minded as we are.

I thought older people were supposed to be wise, but I haven't seen any evidence from them yet.

I fiddle with the cuff of my plaid shirt. It's my favorite: comfortable, worn, and a little too big. I picture my mom's face last night, giving me pleading looks to keep my lips shut. I don't get it.

"Sorry," Dallas whispers, pointing at the song's time on his iPod. It's a billion generations old, but his oldest sister gave it to him before she moved to Australia, so Dallas cherishes it.

"No worries," I reassure him.

Dallas tries to get in at least one song on the ride to my stop, but since he lives so close, he doesn't always get to finish it before I get on. He considers it the best way to set the mood for the day, and it usually tells me how he's feeling.

Today, he's listening to Nat King Cole, and I raise an eyebrow. Nat's his go-to when he needs a pick-me-up. He says it reminds him of his grandmother, and she was the only one who understood him. She passed away two years ago, and I don't think I've heard Dallas sing since.

I wish I could say the same thing about my mom, but she continues to wake me up at the crack of dawn by singing off-key in the shower. It's right beside my bedroom, so I always pull a pillow over my head and beg her to stop.

"Did you remember your permission slip?" Dallas whispers

as he scratches the back of his head. He's still listening to his song when the sun shines through the bus window, making his brown skin glow.

I make a face. Did I? Good question. I start to dig through my backpack, pushing aside some old pieces of paper, a binder, my lunch, and my sweater.

Just as I find it, I notice a large blow-up Mr. Peanut flailing in the wind out the window. I lean forward to get a better look at it. He's massive. I try to calculate approximately how many of me can fit inside him. I'm guessing at least a thousand, but maybe only eight hundred if I'm wearing my blow-up *T. rex* costume from Halloween.

As soon as it's out of sight, I pull out my permission form and flatten it. I wave it in front of Dallas.

He doesn't meet my eyes, so I grab his hand and wrap it in mine. The corner of his mouth briefly twitches into a small smile. I like the contrast of our hands together: his deep brown skin against my sun-kissed white skin. He's not chubby like me, though. He's tall and lanky, especially after he hit a mini growth spurt last year. And Dallas's hair is always neatly trimmed, while I have mastered a classic bedhead look. My hair is short enough that it stands up every which way, but not long enough that I can do anything about it.

When Dallas pulls his hand away, he starts twisting

his headphone cord in his fingers, reminding me of that sunny day.

He had been listening to Keiynan Lonsdale that morning and twisting his headphone cord, just like now. Dallas had never listened to Keiynan Lonsdale before, so I thought that was odd. Then he asked me if we could talk after school.

He didn't make it until then. At lunch, we were settling down in our usual spot in the courtyard, and he blurted, "I'm gay."

I dropped my water bottle, and it rolled under the table. But I left it there so I could hug him tightly and promise that I love him. I'm not entirely sure why, but he got stuck on this idea that I wouldn't want to be friends with him anymore. Coming out is hard, but he never had to worry about me.

"I'm queer too, and I think I want to change my name," I told him, and suddenly, we were a mix of tears and laughter. Dallas shoved my shoulder and teased me about stealing his thunder, but I don't think he felt anything but relief, relief that we were going through this together. At least, I know that's what I was feeling.

Being nonbinary, and figuring it out young, has been a little strange. I know who I am, but I'm unsure how to tell the world. I tested the waters with my name change at school, but so far I've kept my pronouns to a select few: just my mom,

Dallas, and Dallas's family. *Baby steps* is what Dallas calls it. But I don't know anyone who is out in Aberdeen Falls—or the neighboring town, Rose Creek.

Mom is worried about my grandparents. She thinks gender beyond the binary is too much for them. She's probably right, but sometimes I wish for her to be wrong.

What if they can learn just like she did?

Dallas hasn't told his family anything, and I don't blame him. He's afraid one of his sisters would accidentally let it slip or be overheard by his parents. And really, who knows how they'd react? They're cool with me, but I'm not one of their kids. Dallas has five sisters, four of them older, and their parents named them all after places. I think it's a cool way to connect them, but Dallas thinks it's stupid.

It's good that Dallas and I found each other. He gets lost in the shuffle of his family. Sometimes I wonder if his Song of the Day is so vital to him because it's the only time he has alone.

Dallas stops twisting his cord and turns his iPod off when the song ends. He leans back and looks at me.

"What happened?" I ask, hoping the answer is better than I'm expecting.

It's not.

"The usual. Fighting. Screaming. Aspen was crying and

spent the night in my bed again." Dallas runs his hand over his buzzed hair. "I didn't sleep much. Jersey even came and camped out on the floor."

It must have been pretty bad if Jersey left her room. I keep my voice low. "I'm sorry, Dal. Is there anything I can do?"

"Nah," he says, as usual. Some days I wish he'd tell me there *is* something I can do just so I can feel more useful than this.

"Do you want to talk about it or be distracted?"

"Distracted." He rubs his face and then asks, "You had dinner with the grand-ghosts last night. How'd that go?"

I give him a tight smile and lift my hand to start counting on my fingers. "Let's see. They referred to my gender assigned at birth as a weird term of endearment seven times before dessert. Only twice after. They misgendered me the entire night. It's all I could hear ringing in my ears. They called me by my deadname *thirty-two* times. Like, I *know* they don't know my name is Jude now, so of course they'll keep using the name Mom gave me, but . . ."

"Still sucks." Dallas nudges me with his elbow. He whispers, "Jude, Jude, Jude, Jude, Jude, Jude . . ."

I count in my head.

He says my name thirty-three times.

I feel a tear in the corner of my eye, but I don't rush to brush it away. Instead, I let it slip down my cheek and fall

6

onto my chest. It darkens the light orange tank top under my plaid shirt, but I don't care. I lean into Dallas.

"I love you, Dallas Knight."

"I love you too, Jude Winters."

Thirty-four.

CHAPTER 2

Aberdeen Memorial School's seventh grade is big enough to be split into two classes. Thankfully, Dallas and I ended up together. They must have learned that we come as a package deal after my mother asked for me to be switched into Dallas's class last year. The school said Dallas and I should branch out, meet new people, and socialize more. However, my mom argued that they should be fostering strong, stable, and healthy relationships. She won.

We even sit together in every class, except English and science. Mrs. Bayley, our English teacher, assigned seating at random and refuses to let anyone change seats. So Dallas sits at the front of the classroom by the door, and I'm stuck in the last row by the windows.

It wouldn't be so bad if someone other than Stevie Morgan sat beside me.

"Ha," Stevie murmurs.

She's *always* on her phone, and she makes reaction noises to whatever texts she gets, like snickers, giggles, and scoffs. And then she *must* flip her hair over her shoulder every two minutes, as if someone could forget she's blond now.

Like, *we get it already—you have long, beautiful blond hair! You learned how to use makeup in fifth grade! You're Popular.*

"What are you looking at?" Stevie hisses when she notices me watching. I can't help but stick my tongue out in response.

She's never been outwardly mean to me, so I'm not sure why she irks me so much. But I remember a time when she was just Stevie Morgan, star soccer player: fearless, ruthless, and strong. She gave *two* girls bloody noses before third grade. Stevie claimed they were accidents, but who really knows? She was fierce on the field, totally focused and determined to win.

Then Tessa St. James decided Stevie was above all that.

A single summer passed, and Stevie came back in fifth grade with highlights, a new wardrobe, and a new attitude. She quit soccer and learned how to put on fake nails. Sometimes she watches makeup and hair tutorials on her phone in class. Those days make me want to throw it across the room. It's totally rude.

Today her hair flipping is on another level, not to mention the buzzing of her text messages. The blatant disrespect for Mrs. Bayley has me on edge. Sure, English isn't everyone's favorite subject, and some people find it harder than others, but I've seen the 90s come back on Stevie's book reports.

She's *great* at English, so it's not a far reach that she might actually enjoy it too. If I were her, I would be soaking in the lessons and . . .

I realize I'm not her, and I'm not paying attention to Mrs. Bayley myself. At the very least, Stevie could stop being so distracting. She's tapping out messages so fast it makes me wonder if she ever stops.

I glance across the room to see Tessa typing just as fiercely. Doesn't Mrs. Bayley notice them texting?

I wish I could share a look with Dallas. He'd know how I feel, and he'd sympathize.

I narrow my eyes and stare at the back of his head. Maybe he'll somehow hear the silent screaming in my brain and turn around. It sucks when he doesn't get the message and continues writing notes. Maybe he's drawing me a little lizard—he likes to do that sometimes.

Giving up on the mind reading, I lean back in my chair and try to concentrate.

Stevie goes still, *finally*, and yet . . . I can't stop stealing glances at her. She starts to make herself smaller, ducking her head so her hair covers part of her face. Her phone is blowing up with messages, but she's stopped typing out quick responses. Could Tessa St. James's sidekick finally be paying attention?

I try not to focus too much on Stevie, but rather on Mrs. Bayley sketching something out on the chalkboard. She never uses the SMART Board, even though they installed it two years ago. I think she enjoys the chalk's feel in her hand, because she plays with it even when she's not using it.

"Stevie?" Mrs. Bayley says, and I'm sure she asked a question before that, but I have no idea what it was.

I shrink a little in my seat, just in case she's looking for other people to call on.

Stevie lifts her head, and her face has lost all its color. Some of her lip gloss is smudged. She nudges her phone inside the desk, and I watch it light up again, the messages piling in.

I'm not close enough to read them, but the number of notifications is giving me anxiety.

"Sorry," Stevie says, her voice cracking. She tries again. "Could you repeat the question?"

Mrs. Bayley does, and Stevie begins to stammer through an answer. She usually has a straightforward, no-nonsense tone, but right now she sounds small.

Her eyebrows come together as she concentrates on her answer. I cringe, wishing I could help her, but it's too late.

Mrs. Bayley sighs. "That's not the answer I was hoping for, Miss Morgan. Please try to pay attention from now on. Can anyone give me a different answer?"

Tessa's hand shoots up in the air, and she tosses a snotty look in our direction.

Stevie drops her head to scroll through her notifications. She locks the screen, shoves her phone back into the desk, and meets my eyes.

"*What* are you looking at, Jude?"

My lips part. For all the ugly that comes with being part of the Popular Pack, Stevie doesn't deadname me. I came back the September of sixth grade as Jude, and she's never used it against me. Some people had a hard time adjusting to it—especially the teachers—but most switched easily and didn't look back. I didn't broadcast the reason why; that feels private, for those who are worthy of knowing me.

I shake my head, unsure how to ask if she's okay. I don't even know if I want to know the answer anyway.

She turns her attention back to the front of the class, and her eyes don't wander anymore. Stevie doesn't flip her hair or check her phone. Instead, she sits stiffly and scribbles down the odd note here and there.

I'm not sure what I'm supposed to have learned by the end of class, but I notice that before leaving, Stevie shoves her phone into her pocket without checking it. She darts out of the room without acknowledging anyone.

Things are definitely weird with Stevie, but now

that I have the freedom of lunch, I'm not sure I care.

I fall in step with Dallas in the hallway and ask, "So, what'd you draw for me today? A lizard shopping for yogurt? Or maybe wearing a bandanna from the nineties?"

Dallas laughs and shakes his head. "Actually, I was taking notes. I need all the help I can get for the test next week and—"

"Oh no." I put my hand on his arm. "Can I copy your notes? I couldn't pay attention *at all*."

"Having a foggy day?"

Dallas knows I struggle to keep my ADHD in check, even with the medications I'm on. Getting diagnosed two years ago was both a pain and a gift—mostly, though, it allowed me to have a name for the things that feel out of my control. Like spending the entire class fixated on Stevie instead of listening to Mrs. Bayley. Having foggy days where things don't make sense or I can't follow what's being said—that's an ADHD thing. It's weird not being able to control my brain, but it feels better with a reason. Before I just felt lost and confused a lot.

"Something like that," I answer. There's no way I'm going to tell him I was fixated on Stevie. He'll tease me for having a crush on her or something, and I really don't. Stevie is everything I never want to be.

"I'm going to the bathroom first," Dallas says, before dipping into the boys' bathroom.

"Oh-kay," I say to myself, pushing open a cafeteria door. I make my way to our usual seats.

Everything seems fine until Dallas comes to the table looking sick.

"What's wrong?" I ask.

"You're never going to believe what I just overheard."

And he's right—I almost don't believe him.

CHAPTER 3

I lift my hand and shake my head. "Wait, what? Sorry, can you repeat that?"

"Stevie Morgan was kicked out of Tessa's clique," Dallas whispers, double-checking that no one overheard him. Honestly, I don't know why he bothers. No one pays much attention to us anyway. Besides, this is *big* news. It'll make the rounds quick enough.

"I can't believe that," I say, but then I remember how she stopped replying to messages. "Whoa, I think I might have seen the moment it happened, actually."

After explaining what I saw in class, I shrug.

"That's not the shocking part, though," Dallas says, meeting my eyes. His expression is grave, and I can't imagine what he could possibly say to make me care about Stevie's social status.

I almost say as much before he continues.

"Apparently she has a crush on Valencia Bohan."

My stomach sinks.

"I don't know if it's connected. Cass was speculating when I overheard him. But if it is . . ." Dallas swallows.

I look around, trying to spot Stevie, but I can't find her anywhere. My eyes meet Dallas's, and I play with the chain around my neck. "Dallas . . ."

"I had a feeling you'd feel that way," Dallas says, nodding. "I think so too. Go find her."

I don't have to ask him what he means because I already know we're on the same page. After a quick, awkward over-the-table hug, I rush toward the supervising teacher.

I don't make it all the way there before I have an idea. Brownies are always good, and my mom's have gotten me through some rotten days. I dart back to the table, only to find Dallas already holding the brownie outstretched toward me.

"I love you," I say, grinning. He knows me *so* well.

"Love you too," he answers.

When I tell the supervising teacher I have to go to the bathroom, he doesn't even look up from his book. Before I leave the cafeteria, I glance over my shoulder. I spot Tessa tossing her head back and laughing with her other friends, looking unconcerned about Stevie.

• • •

I try three bathrooms before I find Stevie. Now that I'm here, I'm not entirely sure what to do. I only ever use the single-stall gender-neutral bathroom by the gym.

And I have to ask myself, am I the right person to be here?

16

Stevie doesn't have anyone else right now. Tessa and her followers are probably still laughing in the cafeteria as if nothing's wrong. As if their friend hiding in the bathroom isn't their concern. It doesn't feel right to me, so how could it feel right to them?

Dallas and I *always* have each other when things get rough.

I clear my throat, and nothing comes out.

"What do you want, Jude?" Stevie asks from the stall, between sniffs.

I take a step back. "How did you know it was me?"

"I could see your dumb combat boots." There's shuffling inside the stall before the door swings open. Stevie's eyes are red and puffy, and she sniffs louder this time. "So, what do you want? And what are you doing in this bathroom? Everyone knows you only use the single one, for whatever reason."

"You don't need to be *rude*. I don't see anyone else coming to check on you," I snap. I want to slap a hand across my mouth and take the words back, but then I see the smallest tick of amusement in Stevie's eyebrows. It's enough to tell me she didn't take it personally. Softer now, I ask, "Do you want me to go?"

Stevie's eyes seem to bore into me before she nods toward my hand. "Depends. Are you sharing that brownie?"

"Depends," I counter. "Are you going to be nice to me?"

Stevie shrugs, as if the answer doesn't matter. "It beats being mean, I guess. So, *why* are you checking on me?"

"Because," I say, as if that answers her question. She doesn't push me, and I unwrap the brownie. I try to think of something that isn't *because no one should feel alone because of who they like* or *because no one should feel alone at all*. Instead, I find myself saying, "I know Tessa unfriended you. Your friends are jerks."

She hesitates. "They aren't so bad. I don't know why they're doing this . . . I thought they'd understand at least *a little*."

"And they should've understood. There's nothing wrong with you." I hold the brownie out to her and wait. Stevie tilts her head as if she needs to study me, then gently breaks a piece of the brownie off. I can't make myself look at her as I say, "So, I know it's, like, a thousand drops on your social ladder, but you can always hang out with Dallas and me. You don't have to be alone."

"Really?"

"Yeah," I answer, shifting on my feet. I gesture around the bathroom. "I think it *might* beat hanging out by yourself in here, but . . . I guess you'll have to be the judge of that."

"Ha." Stevie takes a bite of the brownie, and I watch my mom's magic happen. She closes her eyes. "Holy crap, Jude. This is the best brownie I've ever had."

"I know. My mom's a witch," I joke. Stevie smiles, meeting

18

my eyes. Her stare is intense, but I can't make myself look away. "You know where to find me."

"That I do," Stevie murmurs. She lifts the brownie. "And I might have become obsessed with these."

Impulsively, I shove the rest into her other hand. "Here, take it all."

"What—I—"

"It's fine," I say quickly. My heart is thudding against my chest, and I swear I can hear it in my ears. Suddenly, it feels like the walls are moving closer to me. I've been in this bathroom far too long. "I've got to get back to Dallas. Sit with us if you want. We aren't jerks."

"Jude—"

"No pressure," I interrupt, taking a step back. "See you around, Stevie Morgan."

"Jude, wait—"

But I can't stay in that bathroom anymore. It feels as though the walls are closing in and I can't breathe. I dart into the hallway and have to rest beside some lockers a few classrooms away. I put my hand to my chest and glance behind me.

I don't know what that was, but it's far too much for me to deal with.

So, I rush back to Dallas. At least with him at my side, I'll be able to calm down.

CHAPTER 4

I don't know what I expected. Maybe for Stevie to start hanging around us? Or at least some acknowledgment of our moment in the bathroom? It doesn't come, and I don't know what to make of that. Dallas doesn't think it's a big deal, but I'm not sure. It feels like one.

"Look," I say to Dallas nearly a week later. Stevie's walking down the hall toward us, ducking her face to avoid making eye contact with everyone whispering as she passes. Her blond hair is pulled up in a messy bun instead of being pin straight, and she's dropped the makeup and trendy outfits for an old band T-shirt and leggings.

"She looks different," Dallas comments, as if it's not obvious. We share a look and then turn back to my locker, letting Stevie pass us in peace.

I'm about to say something else when I see Valencia walk up to her. Their conversation looks tense and uncomfortable. Stevie catches me staring, and embarrassment floods through me. But then she gives me a small up-nod, which I manage to return.

So, maybe we've come to some sort of silent understanding. Like, Stevie knows I'll be there for her if she needs a friend, and I know she'll come to me if she wants to? As confusing as that feels, I'm not sure there's much I can do about it.

• • •

Dallas used to join us sometimes for dinner with my grandparents, but this year, he has to watch his little sister, Aspen, most nights while his parents are at work. Now I'm here on my own, anxiously texting Dallas and hoping he'll distract me enough that I won't have to spend much time actually socializing with my grand-ghosts. Except he doesn't reply, and Mom tells me to put away my phone.

"It's rude," she whispers, giving me *that* look. I grumble, but I put my phone in my pocket anyway. "Set the table, please."

While I'm putting cutlery down, I attempt to start a conversation with my grandparents. "We're going to the Rose Creek Apiary on Friday," I announce.

"Oh, that'll be nice," Nan says. "There's so much to do there. The bees, the lavender fields, the apple orchard, the pumpkin patch . . ."

"Yeah! I'm excited to pick some apples. Dallas is going to take some photos of me, so I'll be sure to show you next Monday."

"You better!"

I smile at her before I glance into the living room at Pops. He either didn't hear me or doesn't care. A fork falls onto the table, as if my hands forgot what they were doing and just let go. I wince, but no one seems to notice.

"I always love the apple orchard in the fall," Nan continues, as if nothing's wrong. She sets a dish of green beans on the table and gives me a wink. "You'll have lots of fun, I'm sure."

"Yeah, should be fun." I try to cover any disappointment I feel about Pops ignoring me and plaster a smile on my face. "How's the office?"

Nan beams at my false interest in her part-time job and starts chattering about an issue she had last week. Mom responds to her, and the conversation moves between them.

I feel my phone vibrate in my pocket and sneak a peek at it.

DALLAS (6:24 PM)

sorry jude! just saw these now. hope tonight goes okay

<3 love u

ME (6:25 PM)

same old, same old . . . love u too!

• • •

I hear Pops curse in the living room while I'm helping Mom and Nan clear the table after dinner. "This darn thing won't work."

"What's wrong, Dad?" Mom calls out.

"The game is on and the cable's out." Pops sighs heavily. "**Jude**, grab your coat. I need you to hold the ladder while I fix the satellite."

I glance toward my mom at the sound of my deadname, but she doesn't seem to react. Instead, she picks up some more dishes and nods toward the living room.

"Go help Pops."

"But—" I start to protest, because setting and clearing the table has always been my main chore. Mom huffs, and I toss my hands up in the air. "Okay, okay. I'm going."

"Thanks, **Jude**," Nan says when she comes back into the dining room. "You know how important the game is to Pops."

I shove my hands into my pockets.

Mom and Nan start chatting about another work story as I walk down the hall toward the front door. I pull on my jacket and slip my shoes on.

"Hurry up with that or else I'll miss the game," Pops says, stepping outside into the cool air. "It's going to be a good one too."

I follow him to the detached garage at the back of the property and watch as he yanks the old door open. It creaks as it slides up. I haven't been inside the garage in a while, because it's off-limits unless Pops is there.

When I take a look around, I realize he's reorganized it since I've been in here last. The place is neater than the house; everything has its home. I'm surprised when I see a shiny electric saw on his worktable.

"Oh, wow! Is this new?" I ask. "Can you show me how it works?"

"Maybe another time," Pops answers. He nods toward the ladder leaning against the wall. "Help me with this, **kid**."

I try to hide my disappointment, but I'm not entirely sure what my face says. I put my hands on one end of the ladder, and Pops lifts up his end. I struggle a bit to keep up as we walk out of the garage.

After we've set the ladder up against the front of the house, Pops gives me a stern look. "This is important, okay? You're going to hold the ladder while I climb up."

"Yes, sir," I say, saluting. His expression doesn't change.

"This isn't the time for jokes," Pops says. "All you kids do these days is make jokes. The game is *on* right now, and I'm missing it. I need you to focus, please, **Jude**."

I'm unsure what to say to that, so I just grip the ladder as tight as I can. He starts up it and carefully climbs onto the roof.

"All right, I'm going to move the satellite, and you're going to look in the window and let me know if the picture is clear or not," Pops calls down. He climbs out of sight, and I take a deep breath.

I peer into the window where I can see the TV screen the best. It's still fuzzy.

"How about now?" Pops calls out.

"Nope," I shout back. We do this a few times before I notice the picture coming in perfectly clear. "All good!"

"Great," Pops says. A few seconds later, he appears at the top of the ladder. "You got it, **kid**?"

I grip the ladder tightly. "Got it!"

He starts to climb down, and when he gets to the bottom, he peeks into the window to see the TV screen. "Now that's what I'm talking about!"

I smile at him, but I don't feel particularly joyful. I know he's going to go back to watching sports while Nan, Mom, and I talk or play a card game. He never wants to spend time with me.

We carry the ladder to the garage. I sneak another glance at the saw.

"Good job," he says, clapping me on the shoulder after we set it down. Sometimes I think he wishes I were someone else. But I'm not. I'm just me. And sometimes me doesn't feel good enough.

I give him a small smile and then trail slowly behind him as we walk back to the house.

Once we're inside, he settles into his usual spot in the living room without another word and I make my way to the dining room.

"How'd it go?" Mom asks as she sits down.

"Fine," I say, shrugging.

"Your mother and I were thinking of playing a card game. Did you want to join us?" Nan asks.

"Sure."

I take my seat and press my lips together. The tension in my shoulders that I brought into this dinner hasn't gone away. If anything, it feels like it's settling in for a long time.

CHAPTER 5

Later that week, Mrs. Reynolds asks to speak with Dallas after class, so I'm waiting near his locker and staring at my phone. The only people I really text are Dallas and Mom, and they're both busy, so I scroll through social media instead.

"Hey, hey, hey," Dallas says, rushing up to me. He swings an arm around my shoulder. "How's Jude?"

"Good . . . What's gotten into you?" I ask. He pouts for a split second and then holds up a piece of paper. I peer at it. "You got an A!"

"I did. Mrs. Reynolds wanted permission to read my health report to the class *and* keep it as an example of what she's looking for in future projects!" Dallas says, grinning. "Apparently she really liked that I chose to write about why queer health is just as important as regular health. Well, straight health."

I grin. "I knew you would ace it. That's awesome, Dal."

"Yeah. I'm pretty happy. And I'm super stoked for tomorrow."

"The field trip?" I ask. We walk down the hall toward

27

the bus parking lot. "It'll be pretty. Promise to take photos of me?"

Dallas sighs. "Of course. I'm your personal photographer. That's all I've ever wanted to be."

I gently shove him. "I fully plan to take photos of you too, with your hat on backward, and those skinny jeans you think you look good in."

"Hey!" Dallas protests. "I *do* look good in those jeans."

I laugh, and we hook arms. As we get on the bus, I say hi to our driver, Mei, an almost-retired Chinese woman with graying hair and the best smiles.

"Good afternoon, Mei!" I say.

"Good afternoon, Jude. Dallas. Hope you kids had a good day," she says with a wink.

We both smile and chat with Mei a little more before walking down the aisle and falling into our usual seat across from Shelby and Kandace.

"Did you see Mr. Garcia's long pink hair today?" Dallas asks, settling in. He nudges me over a bit and then peers out the window.

"I didn't, but I'm sure he looked cool." I nudge Dallas back. "Have . . . *things* gotten better at home? I noticed you were listening to Sam Smith this morning."

Dallas gives me a pointed look. "C'mon, you know it sucks.

Screaming matches, getting in trouble for stuff I didn't do, wishing I could be anywhere but there . . . same thing, different day."

"Sorry."

"It's okay," Dallas says.

"But props to you for listening to a nonbinary icon," I say, gently teasing him.

He gives me a small smile. "Anytime. Oh! I finished the new Robin Hood book last night!"

"No spoilers! I'm on the last chapter!" I protest.

"You'll never guess who dies . . ." Dallas playfully elbows me, and we both start laughing.

"No, no, no!"

From there, we spend the rest of the bus ride dissecting the book in all its glory. Dallas manages not to spoil it for me, but he makes me promise to finish the last chapter tonight.

• • •

The next morning, our class loads onto the bus to go to the apiary. We're going to learn about bees and other insects. I'm excited because the apple orchard is pretty, and it's a change from the day-to-day at school. I was even more excited for the lavender fields, but Mr. Garcia told us yesterday they were harvested in August.

Dallas and I sit together on the bus, in a seat behind Stevie, who doesn't say a word the entire drive. We play I Spy and the license plate game to pass the time. It's not too far a drive, and soon enough we're piling out of the bus and into a small building.

At the far end, there's an entire wall of glass that displays a bunch of beehives. I grab Dallas's arm and drag him over to see.

"I hate bees," he mutters.

"Who cares? This is so cool—you can see everything!" I counter.

A small woman claps to get our group's attention. She's wearing a simple black outfit and a funny-looking hat. It takes me a second, but I realize her hat is striped yellow and black, with two huge black antennas that bobble when she talks. It's a bee hat. She's wearing a bee hat.

I love this place already.

"Hi, everyone. My name is Carrie-Ann, and I'll be your guide today. Welcome to the Rose Creek Apiary and Apple Orchard. We're so happy to have you here with us." She puts her hands on her hips. "First things first, I want to tell you some cool facts about bees, as they are some of our biggest pollinators."

"I'm so happy," I whisper to Dallas. He smirks and nudges me to be quiet.

I watch some bees buzz around their hives as Carrie-Ann talks. "There are twenty thousand known distinct species of bees around the world. And scientists have found fossilized bee nests that are over one hundred million years old."

My lips part in surprise.

"Something else that's cool about bees is they have *five* eyes. They're also smart. In fact, they're so smart that studies show they can recognize faces, and they've even been used for detecting bombs."

"Whoa," I murmur.

Stevie's suddenly beside me, and she gives me a small smile. She leans into me and whispers, "Look at that really fat one."

I follow her pointed finger and see the fattest bee I've ever seen. We share a soft laugh and watch the guy fly away out of sight. I have no idea what Carrie-Ann has been saying since Stevie appeared, even though I try to pay attention. It's not easy when there are so many distractions around, but I try to tune back in.

"There are often symbiotic relationships between pollinators and plants. So, specific pollinators and specific plants help one another. Can anyone think of an example?"

"Like a squash bee?" Shelby asks. *Who even knew there was a squash bee?*

Tessa rolls her eyes, then turns to mutter something to her

friends. Shelby looks a little embarrassed for knowing about squash bees, but Carrie-Ann doesn't seem to notice.

"Exactly! Squash bees pollinate squash. What else?"

I tune out again when Stevie taps my shoulder. She points at a poster, and we giggle at the joke. It reads *Let's get ready to bumble!* and has a funny-looking cartoon bee with its arms up in fists.

I share a quick *what's happening right now?* look with Dallas before pointing out another funny poster to Stevie.

Soon we're whispering about the bees, watching them come into and out of the hives, while Carrie-Ann takes us through their process. Our class listens quietly until Carrie-Ann says, "All right, so before we take a little break, I have one final question. Can anyone tell me what we can do to help pollinators?"

A hand goes up. With a smugness in her voice, Tessa says, "Plant a garden?"

"Yes! Exactly. Planting and tending to a garden is a fantastic way to help our pollinators. Growing veggies or native flowers is perfect. After all, that's how they're pollinated."

I glance at Stevie. She looks a little lost, as if she's not sure where she fits in now. She tucks a piece of hair back from her face.

"Okay, you can go explore the apple orchard now,"

Mr. Garcia announces. "Then we're going to come inside and learn some more things about pollinators and their ecosystems. After that, we'll have lunch, do an activity Carrie-Ann has for us, visit the pumpkin patch, and then head back to the school."

I dart into the orchard while Dallas meanders somewhere behind me. The red apples look so delicious with the sun shining down on them from high in the blue sky.

It's not long before I spot Stevie hovering nearby—alone. I glance around to see Tessa a few rows away, and as soon as I make eye contact with Stevie, she rushes over. She doesn't even try to be casual.

"Jude?"

"Yeah?" I ask, turning my attention back to the apples. I walk between two rows, with Stevie beside me.

"Wait."

I turn to look at her. She pulls at her thin sweater, hugging it tight to her chest, and takes a deep breath. "I wanted to ask you . . . Does your offer still stand?"

"To be friends?" I ask as she rubs her forearms and shifts on her feet. She nods, but she can't meet my eyes. "Yeah, the offer still stands. There's no time limit on it."

"Good," she says, visibly relieved.

"Okay." I'm not sure what else to say.

"Is Dallas okay with me hanging out with you two?" she asks when he starts jogging over.

"Yeah," I say, smiling at him. "Dallas is okay with it. But what changed? I sort of thought you didn't want to be friends."

"Well, I heard you playing the license plate game this morning . . ." Stevie trails off. "It seemed fun. And I'm tired of eating lunch alone."

"Okay," I say, with a nod.

"Okay?" Stevie echoes, as if she's confused.

"Want me to take your photo now?" Dallas asks when he gets to us. He gives Stevie a quick glance before adding, "I can take yours too, Stevie."

"Oh, uh. Thanks."

"Stevie's our friend now," I announce to Dallas. Stevie shoots me a look, but I don't know what it means. "And yes to photos, but I think you should stand over here. The lighting's better on my left side."

Dallas laughs and tells Stevie, "You'll get used to them . . . eventually."

Just like that, we become friends in the apple orchard with the hot sun shining down on us.

CHAPTER 6

When we get back from having an awesome field trip, the three of us head into the school together to pick up our stuff before going home. Dallas motions for me to move out of the way so he can open his locker. He shoves some papers onto the top shelf while Stevie leans against the locker beside his.

"Do you want to hang out with us tonight?" Dallas asks Stevie.

I want to tell Dallas it's *way* too soon for that, but when I catch the look of hope on Stevie's face, I can't let her down. She must have been lonely these past couple of weeks.

"Um, what are you doing?" Stevie asks.

"Babysitting my sister," Dallas answers. A textbook falls from his locker, so I bend down and put it back into place. "But she'll watch TV. She just can't be home alone yet."

"Would that be okay with you, Jude?"

I swallow hard, as if there's something lodged in my throat. I nod and watch Stevie's face light up. She pulls her phone out. "Let me text my parents to let them know where I'll be."

Dallas gives me a look, and I don't even need to ask him

what it means. I lightly step on his foot so he knows to quit it. But his eyebrows are wiggling, and I resist sticking my tongue out at him. It feels like we have our own language sometimes. He nudges his shoe against mine, and I shoot him a pointed stare.

Honestly, now is not the time or place.

Did I have a little crush on Stevie back when she was running around the soccer field, giving girls bloody noses? *Maybe.* But it was mostly because I thought she was so hardcore. She seemed so secure and sure of herself. And at the time, I hadn't known if I wanted to be *with* her or *be* her. It's still strange to me how quickly a summer can change things, and how quickly crushes can end.

"Cool. I'm all set," Stevie announces.

"You don't need to go to your locker?" I ask.

Stevie shakes her head. "Nope. I packed up all my stuff and brought it with me on the trip."

"Why?" Dallas says, tilting his head. I nudge him with my elbow, but he just gives me a confused look.

"Oh, um. Tessa's locker is close by, so . . ." Stevie trails off.

"Let's go!" I say, hoping to move past the awkward moment.

Then we're heading to the buses together, and I feel a little dumbfounded by the whole situation. It doesn't feel real.

Stevie gently bumps my side and gives me a curious expression. "You okay there, Jude?"

I don't want to admit it, but I will here, where no one else will ever hear it: I love how often she uses my name.

"Yep. You?"

"I'm okay." Her smile is beautiful as it spreads across her face, and somehow it eases the tension in my shoulders. Her eyes twinkle when she says, "You're going to regret offering to be my friend."

"Yeah?"

"Yep. Your social status is going to plummet *so* hard," Stevie answers. "Think you can handle that?"

I laugh harder than I expect. "What world do you live in where *we* care about that?"

Stevie's eyebrows jump, but she doesn't comment on that. Instead, she asks, "Hey—don't I need a note to get on your bus?"

"Usually, yeah, but Mei likes me. Watch me charm her."

"You? Charming?" Dallas asks, snorting. "You wish."

I roll my eyes at him and stage-whisper to Stevie, "Mei also accepts text messages in place of notes."

Stevie laughs, and I like the way her face lights up. I ignore Dallas's expression of amusement because he's probably reading my mind right now, but Stevie doesn't seem to notice.

Mei reads the message from Stevie's parents and says, "Happy to have you on board, Miss Stevie. You're hanging around these two jokers?"

"She might not admit it," I say from behind Stevie, "but we're totally Mei's favorite students."

"Well, your mother's chocolate brownies might have something to do with that," Mei says, winking at us.

"I'll be sure to let her know the bribes are working." That makes Mei laugh a full-belly-type laugh, and she tips her imaginary hat to me.

I gently nudge Stevie forward, and she follows Dallas down the aisle. He takes our usual seat, and I nod toward the empty one across from him. Shelby and Kandace will have to find somewhere else to sit today. Stevie settles in against the window, and I tuck my feet in from the aisle to let someone pass.

"So . . ." Stevie says, rubbing her thighs.

"So," Dallas echoes.

"I liked Mr. Garcia's wig today," I announce, and watch as they both look relieved. "But my favorite is the bubblegum-pink one he wore last year. It was like a little bob, and he had a Hello Kitty clip in it. It weirdly suited him, to be honest."

"I'm not over the Thor wig he wore on the first day of school," Dallas says, grinning. "So. Cool."

"I liked that one too!" Stevie exclaims.

"He was like a stocky version of Thor! I should've lent him the hammer from my Halloween costume last year," Dallas says, making Stevie laugh.

"My favorite is definitely the Dolly Parton one," Stevie tells us. "I didn't even know who Dolly Parton was until Tessa pointed it out. Her mother is a huge Dolly fan. When she showed me a photo of her, I couldn't unsee it."

"I'm going to google this," Dallas decides. We wait while he searches it up, and then he whistles. "Oh! I know the wig you're talking about now. Mr. Garcia made a great Dolly Parton."

Dallas turns the screen to show Stevie and me. A giggle escapes me almost instantly. "Oh my god! That one looked so ridiculous on him. Does anyone even know *why* Mr. Garcia wears all those wigs?"

"No," Dallas says, shaking his head.

Stevie looks around and lowers her voice, waving Dallas to lean in closer. We're awkwardly huddling in the aisle. "His wife was sick a few years ago and lost all her hair. I guess they invested in a bunch of wigs to cheer her up, and now that she's better, she doesn't wear them anymore. So, Mr. Garcia decided to get some more use out of them."

"Oh," Dallas says. "I had no idea."

I tilt my head to look at Stevie, aware of how close our faces are. "Is that true?"

"That's what my mom told me," Stevie says, leaning back.

Then her expression changes, and she presses a hand to her cheek, covering her mouth slightly. She won't meet my eyes, so I try to share a look with Dallas. Except he's still busy scrolling through photos of Dolly.

I slump back against the seat and quietly ask, "Is everything okay?"

"Yeah, just, uh, thinking about my mom." Stevie shifts again, pulling at the sleeves of her sweater. "Things haven't been great between us since my parents got divorced."

I don't know what to say, so I'm glad when Stevie asks, "Hey, did your mom pack any more brownies?"

"Not today. But Mom makes them almost every other week because she figures it'll make Dallas love her more."

Dallas perks up at the sound of his name. "I would've loved her without the brownies, but they definitely don't hurt. Have you met their mom before, Stevie?"

"Maybe once? I feel like she was at a soccer game or something," Stevie says, shrugging.

"She's really cool," Dallas says.

I beam; Dallas is right. My mom *is* cool.

Stevie and Dallas talk past me while my thoughts get away

from me. I glance at Dallas, and for once, he's not already looking at me. Instead, he's telling Stevie a story and breaks into laughter before he gets to the best part. I smile. He always does that.

Stevie's trying to guess the ending, but Dallas can't manage to spit it out.

I listen to the bits of conversation around me without really soaking them in. Someone's having a great day because they're getting the latest video game from their favorite series; one kid wants to finish their project a whole week in advance so they can hang out with their older brother; another girl is talking about a skateboard trick she learned and showing off her new scar.

"Jude," Stevie says, tugging on my sleeve. "Dallas says it's our stop."

"Oh!"

I jump up, swinging my backpack over my shoulder, and accidentally hit Stevie with it. I give her a quick apologetic smile before taking off down the aisle behind Dallas's sister. I can't believe I zoned out long enough to lose track of time and where we are. Again. For the billionth time. You'd think I'd have a handle on it by now, but nope. *That's* another ADHD thing.

"I'll see what I can do about scoring you some brownies,"

I tell Mei before giving her a wave and jumping off the last step.

Dallas hooks his thumbs behind his backpack straps, waiting beside his sister. "Pen, this is Stevie. Stevie, this is my bratty little sister, Aspen."

Aspen shoots daggers with her eyes, crossing her arms. I swear, no one gives attitude better than Aspen. "I'm *not* bratty!"

"Yeah, yeah," Dallas says. "C'mon, brat. I'll let you watch TV instead of doing homework."

"I'm not bratty," Aspen declares again, this time to Stevie.

She eyes Stevie, and I'm grateful I haven't had to earn Aspen's respect. She's sort of stuck with me since I've known Dallas my whole life. But Aspen is tough on most people.

I have no idea where her innate distrust comes from, but I guess it's not the worst thing. After all, Stevie's friends abandoned her when she needed them. A little distrust might have protected her feelings.

As we walk into Dallas's house, Aspen starts firing questions at Stevie at a rapid speed, but Stevie's impressive. She answers them at the same pace, not missing a beat.

"You're stuck on an island. What three things do you bring with you?"

"A knife, a book, and a floatie."

42

"You are a witch up against a demon, and your wand just broke. What do you do?"

"Sneak up on him and hit him over the head with a frying pan."

"Like Rapunzel in *Tangled*!" Aspen exclaims.

"Yeah!"

"Dallas told you I'm a brat. Do you believe him?"

"No, I like to form my own opinions."

Aspen's expression betrays nothing, but I know Stevie has her approval. Dallas heads into the kitchen, and I'm tempted to follow him just to freak out about the fact that *Stevie Morgan* is here. It feels like a rude thing to do, though, so I stay put.

"Hey, Pen?" Dallas calls.

"What?" Aspen calls back as if it's the biggest chore.

"Do you want a snack before we go upstairs?"

"No!" Aspen settles down on the couch and turns on the TV. She looks over the back of the sofa. "Do you still watch Disney?" she asks Stevie.

"All the time!" Stevie answers brightly. I'm sure she means it too. "It's my favorite channel. Have you seen *Andi Mack*?"

"Yeah! But only 'cause Jude let me borrow the DVDs. I'm sad it was canceled." Aspen glances at the TV. "Okay, I'm going to need everyone to be quiet now."

"I got us some snacks!" announces Dallas, coming back into the living room.

"Quiet!" Aspen calls out.

Dallas rolls his eyes. "Whatever. We're going to be upstairs, okay? Don't let anyone into the house, yell if you need us, and—"

"I'm ten. I think I can handle it," Aspen says, without looking away from the TV. "Pretty sure I'm smarter than you anyway."

I laugh and nudge Dallas in the arm. "I think she has you there, Dal."

"Hey! No ganging up on me in my own home!" Dallas leads the way up the stairs, and Stevie hesitates for just a second before following.

I immediately jump onto Dallas's bed, dropping my backpack to the floor. I grab my body pillow and lie partially on top of it.

Dallas and I don't like sharing the same bed during sleepovers, just because it feels weird. I'm not sure why that changed, to be honest, but I usually take the floor now. The body pillow changed sleepovers for me. I used to *hate* sleeping on the floor, but now I don't actually mind it.

"Wow, your room is . . . interesting," Stevie says as she looks at his wall. His collage of photos is elegant, if I do say so myself. I made it for Dallas's birthday last year. I did papier-mâché with photos of us and his sisters over a science project from sixth grade that we got an A-plus on. It's not my best work since the papier-mâché is a little sloppy, but Dallas proudly hung it in his bedroom.

"It's neat," Stevie decides, looking around some more. "I sort of expected all boys' rooms to be messy."

Dallas laughs. "If you want to see a mess, just go to Jude's bedroom. Their mom says it looks like a tornado hits it about twice a day."

"Hey," I protest, slapping his arm. "It's called organized chaos. *I* know where everything is."

"It's a cry for help," Dallas states. He flops down into his chair. "What's your room like, Stevie?"

"It's pretty clean, but that's because I share it with my sister, and she's a neat freak." Stevie puts on a mimicking voice. *"What do you think you're doing? Pick that up right now. It belongs two inches to the left, and you know it."*

"Oof," I say. Stevie gives me a warm smile and sits on the edge of Dallas's bed. She fidgets with her hands in her lap.

"How have you been?" I ask her. "You know, with everything?"

"Okay, I guess." Stevie shrugs, but I bet it bothers her more than she's willing to admit. "I can't really believe I'm here, to be honest."

"Should we be offended?" Dallas asks, but there's a hint of amusement in his tone. I'm not sure Stevie picks up on it, because she frowns.

"Don't you think it's weird that we're going to be friends?" she asks in response.

"Yeah!" I blurt without thinking. "Who saw *that* coming? Not me."

Stevie's eyes go wide, and I cover my mouth with my hands. I really shouldn't have said that. I'm about to apologize, I swear, because it's rude, but then Stevie starts *laughing*, and I'm at a loss for words.

Stevie's laughing on Dallas's bed, and all I can do is share a dumbfounded look with him before we burst into laughter too.

CHAPTER 7

I really don't know what to think. Hanging out with Stevie is not at all how I thought it would be. In fact, I'm almost tempted to say she's fun. But don't quote me on that just yet. We end up playing some card games and talking about the other people in our class. Stevie knows a lot about our classmates, and it's fun to gossip even if I don't learn anything too scandalous.

Everything's fine until a door slams downstairs; then Aspen walks into Dallas's room. Her lips are pressed together, and I know what that means. Dallas gives me a small nudge on my foot, but I'm already springing into action.

"You know what I want to do? I want to go swing in the park." I clap my hands together and look at Stevie. "What do you think?"

"Oh! Uh, I haven't done that in a long time." Stevie smiles, though, just like I knew she would. No one can resist the swings. "That sounds fun!"

"Cool. Let's go."

"I'm going to stay with Aspen," Dallas says, putting his

hand gently on his sister's shoulder. "Maybe we'll text Jersey and see if she can take us to get ice cream?"

"Okay!"

"Let's hurry," I say, rushing to grab my stuff. I wave my hand to get Stevie to pick up the pace, and she looks at me with confusion. It's not like I can just say, *Hey, so Dallas and Aspen's parents are about to have a huge explosive fight, and we don't want to be here for it! So, move it!*

I give Dallas a quick hug, and he gives me one of those bro pats on the back. He can be weird like that. Then I grab Stevie's wrist and yank her out the front door.

"What's going on?" Stevie whispers, but I ignore her question.

It's not until we're walking past Mrs. Mantle's house that I look back over my shoulder. Almost right on cue, I see Dallas's father pull into the driveway. It'll start in a few minutes if his mother's door slamming is any indication. I pull my phone out to text Dallas that he and his sisters can come to my place if things get terrible. I do that every time, but he never takes me up on the offer because he worries about what my mom will think of his parents.

Dallas says they're not bad people, but the constant arguing over the last few years has made me question it. Their fights never seem to be about important stuff, just little petty things. I'm not sure what changed when Dallas and I were in fourth grade, but they eventually stopped taking us to get ice cream on Haggett Street, which was our Friday-night tradition for as long as I can remember.

I wish it was easier on Dallas, but I do what I can. We usually avoid his parents as much as possible. It helps that Dallas's mom runs a successful business and that his dad is a work-obsessed corporate guy, so neither is home much.

I wait until Dallas texts that he and Aspen are watching Netflix on his laptop before I put my phone away. I know they'll be sitting on the floor with their backs against the bed, pretending the other side of the bedroom door doesn't exist.

I don't really get it. Dallas won't let me tell my mom, but the fighting thing doesn't seem normal. And sometimes they take it out on Dallas, and I *hate* that.

"Jude?"

I look up, surprised to see Stevie and I have already walked all the way to the park. I blink a few times before answering her. "Yeah?"

"Do you think I'm a bad person?"

"What?" The question catches me off guard. I settle onto a swing, and Stevie takes the other. "No, not really."

"But you do a little?"

"Sometimes Tessa and her friends can be, um . . ." I hesitate, but Stevie's expression seems almost hopeful. I don't know how to explain it. My gut tells me she wants me to be honest with her, so that's what I do. "They can be a little exclusive and rude. They make people feel like outcasts or unworthy since they don't let anyone else into their little club. I don't know if I would say that *you* are like that since you're the only one who calls me by the right name, but . . ."

"They're not always nice," Stevie whispers. I glance over at her, surprised to find tears in her eyes. "They don't like people disagreeing with them."

"It must have been really hard."

"It was." Stevie takes a deep breath. "Thank you for understanding. And for offering to be my friend. You didn't have to do that."

"I did," I say. "No one should be friendless."

Stevie lets out a laugh, but it sounds almost hollow. Like it could have its own endless echo. "You're right. But I was friendless. They told me that if I couldn't . . . get over it, then I couldn't be part of the group anymore. They deleted me from the group chats and everything."

"Wow."

"Yeah."

"I'm sorry." It's the only thing I can think to say, but

somehow, it feels like it's the right thing. Stevie gives me an appreciative look, and I decide to change topics. "Dallas and I have rules if you're going to be our friend."

"You do? What kind of rules?"

"You are not allowed to miss Taco Tuesday at my house unless you have a really good reason," I tell her. My voice sounds more confident than I feel. Am I really introducing her to my rules with Dallas already? Isn't this too soon? And yet, my mouth keeps moving. "You must *always* interrupt all conversations to point out any cats or dogs nearby. You must not lie. Not even dumb white lies."

"I really like the taco and animal rules," Stevie says, grinning. "And I think I can manage the honesty one too."

"It's the most important. Dallas and I always have each other's back, so . . . if you're going to be our friend, you must have ours." I take a breath before adding, "And we'll have yours."

Stevie smiles, and things almost feel right in the world. She rocks gently back and forth before coming to a stop on the swing. "I can totally handle that. So, did I pass?"

"What?"

"Was this not a test?" Stevie asks, waving a hand in the air. "To be friends with you or not."

I shake my head. "No? What are you talking about?"

"Oh, I—" Stevie frowns and ducks her head so I can't see her face. I want to reach out to hold her hand or something, but it's too soon for that.

"Did . . . Did they *test* you?"

Stevie nods, keeping her head down. "Yeah. All the time. Tessa said it was to make sure people stayed loyal and . . ."

I hear a sniff, and I get up from my swing. I bend down in front of her so I can look at her face. "Stevie, that's not okay. There are no tests in friendship. You shouldn't have to prove your loyalty or friendship to anyone. Our rules are just for fun."

"I—" Stevie brushes her eyes with the back of her hand. "I don't want to talk about it. Um, I don't mean to pry, but Dallas is okay, right?"

"Oh, uh . . ." I pause, wondering what's the best thing to say. "He's fine."

"Okay."

I don't leave yet. Instead I push back some of Stevie's hair. Dallas does that to me sometimes when I'm crying, and it makes me feel better. Like someone's taking care of me, and I'm not alone. He says it's because he doesn't want my hair to get wet from the tears and stick to my face. But I like it all the same. "I offered to be friends, Stevie. If you accept, then we're friends. That's it. There's no test to pass."

"Just like that?"

"Just like that."

Stevie blinks; her eyes are so damp from crying. Then she lunges forward and tackles me into a hug. I lose my balance, and we both fall backward on the sand. It's okay, though, because Stevie starts to laugh, and I like the sound.

"What was that?" I shout, but I'm starting to laugh now too.

"I'm sorry!" Stevie says between giggles. "I didn't mean to jump you!"

I lie on my back and stare up at the sky. There are big white clouds way above us. I glance over to see Stevie looking up at them as well.

"I really wanted a hug."

I snort. "Yeah, I got that from the tackling."

"I see a pig."

"What?"

"There!" Stevie points toward the sky. "See, that could be a huge snout thing, and then that could be a front leg. But you can totally see the little tail over there."

I squint. "I don't see a pig. But I could definitely make an argument for a lion."

"What?!" Stevie protests. "*How* do you get a lion out of a pig?"

I burst out laughing at her question, and she starts giggling again, and this is the moment that I know it: Stevie is going to change my life.

Nothing is going to be the same, ever again.

I think I'm ready.

CHAPTER 8

It's almost weird how quickly she becomes part of our lives. Within a week, Stevie meets my mom, and they get along too well. Stevie hangs around with Dallas when he babysits Aspen, even on nights I can't make it. Sometimes I wonder if I should be threatened by their friendship, but I've found myself in the park with Stevie more often than not.

Apparently making friends can be that simple.

She becomes such a big part of my life that I'm starting to have a tough time picturing it without her.

I send her a text while I wait for the bus at the end of my driveway. After a moment, the three little dots appear on my screen as I lean against the mailbox. I play with the flag, moving it up and down, and frown when the dots disappear.

A second later, a message from Stevie comes in.

STEVIE (7:34 AM)
Ugh, it is far too early to be awake right now, Jude!!!!!!!!!!

ME (7:34 AM)

looool youre gonna have to get a job that lets you sleep in when we grow up

STEVIE (7:35 AM)

Those exist??? SIGN ME UP FOR THAT KIND OF CAREER

STEVIE (7:35 AM)

Anyway, to answer your original question, no, I can't kill you so you don't have to go to dinner with the grand-ghosts. Murder is highly frowned upon, you know

ME (7:36 AM)

since when do YOU care if something is frowned upon? but fiiiiiine. if i'm mean tomorrow, it's all your fault

STEVIE (7:37 AM)

How dare you blame me for this! Also, I hate that your bus arrives so much later than mine. Why do /I/ have to be at school at 7:35am, and your bus gets in at 7:50am? IT'S HARDLY FAIR

ME (7:38 AM)

lololol hey, I'm not the one who makes the schedule!

Stevie sends me a row of angry and ridiculous emojis just as Mei pulls up. I climb the stairs and pull a brownie from my pocket. She gasps and presses it to her chest.

"I'm in love with your mother, Jude."

I laugh. "That's what everyone says. But I'll let her know you're interested."

Mei laughs too, because we both know she's far too old for my mother. (Not to mention my mother's straight, as far as I know.)

I make my way to my usual seat and slip in beside Dallas. He holds the iPod up so I can see his Song of the Day is a Hayley Kiyoko one from the Queer Anthem playlist we made together. That means he had a good night after I left his house last night.

"I'm going to come out to her," I tell Dallas when he takes his headphones out.

"What?"

"Stevie. I'm going to come out to her."

Dallas gives me a smile. He nudges me with his elbow. "Yeah? Are you hoping . . . ?"

"What? No!" I shake my head. "Dallas, *no*. I don't have a crush on her again. And even if I did, that's not why I want to tell her. She's one of us now, isn't she?"

"Huh." Dallas leans back against the seat. "I never really considered it, but I guess she is. I mean, we talk more in the group chat than in our private chat now."

"Exactly." I give him a bright smile. It's perhaps a little too forced, because Dallas gives me *that* look. I deflate. "What? I just want to send the gay memes to her too."

Dallas snorts. "If *that's* why you want to come out to her, be my guest. But we haven't really been friends with her that long. Are you ready for her to know?"

I tug the sleeve of my favorite plaid shirt. I wore it today as extra armor . . . or maybe for extra comfort. If today's the day I come out to Stevie, I'm going to need it *just in case*, because I can only hope how someone will react.

If it's different, it's scary—at least that's what Mom says whenever I bring up coming out to my grandparents. I don't know how I feel about that, because Dallas is almost my exact opposite, and yet, he's my person. But maybe Mom has a point. People are afraid of what they don't know. And people react poorly when they're scared.

Nodding firmly, I say, "Yes. I'm ready."

"Well, it's not like it'll be a surprise."

I look at him with wide eyes.

Dallas doesn't say anything else, but I know him well enough to know there's more. I wait. He takes a breath and scrunches his nose. "Please don't hate me."

"You told Stevie. How could you?!"

"No! I would *never* out you," Dallas rushes to say. He grabs my hand and squeezes it. "You know I'd never do that to you."

"I guess." I exhale. "But . . . ?"

"Well, it hurts my heart to misgender you, so I kept using your pronouns around her."

I pat Dallas's hand. He's a good one. "I would've told you to misgender me if I was super concerned about it, you know."

"I know. But I should've asked what you wanted me to do."

"It's on both of us for not talking about that earlier," I say. "It's hard not being fully out, but I don't think everyone at school would understand the pronoun thing."

"We don't really know that—they took your name pretty well."

"I guess. Anyway, is that it? You kept using my pronouns with Stevie?"

"And . . . then Stevie asked. And I told her to talk to you," Dallas says. He takes his hand back, but only to grab his water bottle. During tough conversations, Dallas usually gets a dry mouth. He always freaks out when I bring him water, because he knows it means I want to talk about something serious.

"Oh. What did she say?"

"That she would wait until you talked to her." Dallas takes another sip of his water. "So, she's not going to be surprised, and I think she's already pieced it together."

"Well." I consider this. "I guess this might be the easiest coming out I've had yet?"

"I hope so. I told her that if she has a problem with anything, she would be in the bathroom again. And that my loyalties lie with you."

"Dallas!" I frown at him.

"What?"

"You didn't."

"I wanted her to know . . ."

"That she's a disposable friend to you?" I say. "Come on. She's already lost *one* friend group. You can't threaten her with ours too."

"I just thought—"

"Dal."

"Okay. I'll apologize." Dallas rubs his face. "It's weird having another friend. But you're always going to come first, Jude. It just be like that sometimes."

I know, deep down, if I were forced to choose, I would pick Dallas. He's the only person who's willing to call me out when I do dumb things. He's also the only person who doesn't yell at me when I have a terrible night and call him at two o'clock in the morning, crying.

But I hope it never comes down to that because I'm growing to really care about Stevie too. She stuck two straws in her mouth and talked like a walrus the other day at lunch because she thought she saw me frown. I'm fairly sure my face just looks like that, but it made me giggle anyway.

I glance at Dallas and wonder if he understands just how important Stevie is to me. She's (maybe) queer like us. I hope she doesn't feel alone.

I lucked out with Dallas, but what about Stevie? Her friends weren't really friends, after all. I wish I could talk to her about it, but I don't want to force her to come out. She'll tell me when she's ready. But maybe if I tell her that I'm queer too, she'll feel safe enough to share with me.

"Don't come out to her because you want her to come out to you," Dallas says as if he's reading my mind.

"I'm not! Maybe a little! I don't know!"

"Okaaay . . . So, how was dinner with the grand-ghosts last night?" Dallas asks, nudging my hand off his. I pull it back into my lap and don't quite meet his eyes.

I cringe. "They had to reschedule, so it's happening tonight instead of Taco Tuesday. Sorry, but wish me luck surviving, please. The last few have been more of the same."

Dallas waves his hands around as if he's trying to cast a spell on me. "Luck . . . wished!"

I laugh, and any tension between us melts away.

CHAPTER 9

I'm a chicken. Coming out to Stevie turned out to be a lot harder than I expected. I started the day off with so much determination, and then when we had a moment alone at lunch, I hesitated. I couldn't get the words out of my mouth.

Even though she has an idea because Dallas has been using my pronouns, it's still hard. What if she's not supportive? What if she laughs at me or calls me a bad name? What if . . . And the questions keep coming. Coming out could cost us our friendship, despite how close we've grown.

I have no idea what she'll think when I come out. Maybe she'll feel differently knowing the truth.

What if she asks me, *Are you sure?* Because Mom did that at first. I get it now. She was in shock because she hadn't been expecting it.

But those three words haunt me.

Are you sure?

Am I sure I'm not a girl or a boy? Yes.

Am I sure my gender can be described as waving my hands in the air and wanting to scream into a pillow? Yes.

Am I sure I'm worthy of love? Up until that moment, I thought so.

But when Mom asked me, *Are you sure?* I questioned it. Not about being nonbinary. Not about being queer or bisexual. But about whether I was worthy of love. Because if my own mother could doubt me, doubt how I feel, doubt how I *am*, what's stopping anyone else from questioning me or my worthiness? And maybe that's not what she meant to do when she asked me that question, but that's how it felt.

Mom got better, though. She collected herself quickly and told me she loves me, no matter what. But sometimes I wonder if *no matter what* implies that my gender and sexuality is something she thinks I should be ashamed of. Or maybe she's ashamed of me. Like she has to point out that there are no conditions to loving me, but maybe there really are.

It was different with Dallas. He hugged me and said, *I love you so much.* There wasn't a condition attached to it. Not that *no matter what* is really a condition, but . . . it sort of feels like it sometimes. Those words didn't work for me. Maybe someone else can find comfort in *no matter what* but not me.

I always feel a tightness in my chest when I think of Mom's words, and I obsessed over them for a while. It echoes in my mind. *Are you sure? . . . I love you, no matter what.* I tug at my shirt sleeve just thinking about it.

I get that Mom didn't know how to respond. Afterward, she spent hours googling and researching things. She sat me down and gave me this really long, passionate speech. Told me how she loved me and how nothing would ever change that. She asked about hormones and if I wanted to start them. I said no.

My body isn't the problem. How I present myself is. It's expensive to get a whole new wardrobe, and I can't ask Mom to invest any of her savings into fresh clothes. But I'd wear more rompers and pieces that make me feel comfortable if I could. I'll have to wait until I'm older, I guess.

For now, I'm forced to pass as cis, which means everyone still assumes I'm the gender I was assigned at birth, and I'm trying my best to be okay with that.

I wish there were more nonbinary famous people, to be honest—especially ones who are a Confusing Mystery. Because that's my goal: to one day be so confusing that people know I'm not cis, but they're not entirely sure what I am. I want people to know at a glance that I'm *more* than how I look.

On top of that, most nonbinary people I see in photos are skinny, white, and androgynous. I like to tell Dallas I'm comfortable, but the truth is, I'm fat. Being fat makes being a cis-presenting nonbinary person harder. Everyone looks at you and thinks they know exactly who you are.

They put you into these neat little boxes, but I'm a lot messier.

Some days are easier than others. Sometimes when Dallas refers to me as *man*, I get a wave of happiness. Other times, he'll jokingly tell me to *get it, girl*, and I'll laugh with him. I don't know how Dallas does it, but he always manages to understand the gender vibes I'm feeling without me saying a word.

And *that* is what helps me the most on days when being cis-presenting makes my skin itch. Knowing that Dallas will always have my back.

It would be incredible to know Stevie has my back too, but . . . I guess there's never an easy way to come out. It's one giant irreversible decision.

And if it doesn't go well . . .

I sigh heavily.

"What's going on in that head of yours?" Mom asks as she pulls into my grandparents' driveway. There's no escaping this tonight. I begged Mom to let me out of this family dinner, but she said no such luck. If she had to deal with them, so did I. I laughed, but part of me wishes she would've let me stay home instead.

"What?"

"You've been awfully quiet, kid." She leans forward to

look at me. "I know this sucks. I want to protect you, baby. It'll get easier, I promise."

I take a sharp breath. "When?"

"What?"

"When will it get easier?" I ask, rubbing my nose. I refuse to cry. "Because, Mom, it's just getting harder and harder every time we come here. I *hate* having to hide this part of who I am from them."

"Jude . . ."

"I know. I *know*."

"They have outdated views," Mom explains, for the hundredth time. "They won't understand. They might disown you, and I would never forgive myself if you lost your grandparents."

"But . . . would that really be so awful?" I can't look at her when I say this. I don't want to break her heart. These are her *parents*. I couldn't imagine my life without my mother, and I'm sure she feels the same way about my grandparents. I shake my head. "Never mind. Let's get this over with."

"Wait, Jude . . ." Mom puts her hand on my wrist. "Is it really getting worse?"

I nod, barely reaching her eyes now. "It's hard. I know I don't have to come out to everyone. And that it's not always going to be *safe* to come out, but . . . we come here once a week. Am I going to have to pretend every Monday for the rest of my life?"

My mom's lips part, but she doesn't say anything. I put my hand on top of hers.

"It's okay. I can survive a few more years. It's not the end of the world. Really."

"Jude—"

"I love you."

"I love you too, kid." She presses her lips to my forehead. "If you do really want to come out, I will support you."

Read: My mom will choose me over her own parents if she has to. But I don't want her to lose her parents because of me.

I give her a reassuring smile, hoping it looks real; then I push the car door open. Maybe one day I won't have to be terrified to come out to anyone. It just doesn't look like that's going to happen anytime soon.

Nan opens the front door and gives me a huge hug. It feels warm and safe, and for a moment, I can't imagine her rejecting me. But Mom knows best.

Nan always smells like expired perfume. I don't know how else to explain it. I'm sure the fragrance isn't *actually* expired because Pops loves to spoil her, but still.

I take a deep breath when she releases me.

"What's wrong, **child**?" Nan asks, searching my face.

Child isn't the word she uses, but I always correct her in my mind. It's the only way I know how to cope. I shrug and say, "Long day, that's all."

Nan pats my cheek and turns to hug Mom. Then we're rushed into the dining room. I immediately busy myself by focusing on the crossword Nan had started to fill in. Mom and Nan talk as they work on the food. Pops is in the living room watching some game; he doesn't even get up to say hello. It takes everything in me to not roll my eyes.

Pops used to try to get me to watch sports, but he's finally stopped asking. Nan would tell him that I wasn't the type to be into games anyway, and I'm still not sure what that meant. I *could be* if I wanted to, but I'm just not interested in sports. It doesn't have anything to do with my "type."

When Dallas joined us for dinner sometimes, he would pretend to be wholly immersed in the games, just because he gets a kick out of my grandfather. He thinks the tough-guy persona is a ruse for being soft, because he once saw Pops with a stray kitten. Plus, he loves Nan's homemade chocolate chip cookies. But I think that the general calmness of our family is what Dallas likes best.

"Hi, Dad," Mom says. "How are you?"

"Good. Just watching the game," he calls, without tearing his eyes from the TV.

"What's the score?" I ask, feeling awkward. I hover between the living room and the kitchen.

He jumps up to yell something at the TV, and I sigh. Either he didn't hear me or he's ignoring me.

"**Jude**." My grandmother deadnames me. I correct her in my head so I don't say anything rude. I turn and see she's holding up her tablet. "I'm having some issues with this thing. Would you mind helping? Earl can set the table. Earl!"

"Busy!" he shouts back.

I roll my eyes.

Nan sighs and lets it go. "Oh, well, I'll have your mother set it."

"What's the issue?" I ask, biting my tongue about the rest.

Nan gives me a long, rambling explanation of the problem she's having with her tablet. It's not something I really know about, but I figure I can play around with it.

I take the tablet into the living room and sit down. After a few minutes, I look up from fiddling with its settings to see Pops shouting at the TV, Nan pulling a dish out of the oven, and Mom setting the table. I get a weird urge.

One I should probably ignore.

But after I fix Nan's tablet, I open up the internet browser, type in my search, and click on a link.

Let's Talk About Being Nonbinary.

I stare at it. I skim the article. It talks about gender, pro-nouns, what it means, and how to support nonbinary pals. It seems like a good starting point for someone who wants to learn.

Even if it's just me who wants them to learn.

And then I minimize the tab.

CHAPTER 10

I've tried to come out to Stevie seven more times. Dallas tells me to take it as a sign that I'm not ready, and that Stevie isn't in any rush to know. He's probably right, but sometimes I wish I had more than just Dallas to talk about these types of things with.

Dallas is okay with no one else knowing he's gay. He doesn't feel the deep, gnawing feeling that I do. I hate keeping secrets. I hate hiding part of who I am. And I want to be free of this weight I carry with me like a backpack I can never put down.

"Jude?" Stevie asks, bringing her swing to a stop. We left Dallas's house when his parents came home, but Stevie's mother can't pick her up until eight, so we have two hours to chill in the park. We're both having late dinners tonight. I would invite her over to my place, but my room is *extra* messy, and Mom would have a fit if Stevie saw it like that.

"Yeah?" I ask, slowing my swing down.

"Thanks, um. Thanks for being my friend." Stevie tucks a piece of hair behind her ear. She's wearing a pair of leggings and one of Dallas's hoodies, but it's baggy on her. She has Converse shoes on, and I'm shocked she even knows what they are. Tessa is all about cute sandals and boots. "I'm not always good at emotions or anything, but . . . I really appreciate it. I thought I was going to be all alone, and . . ."

I skid my swing to a stop and reach out to grab her hand. She looks up at me with surprise.

"Hey. It's okay," I say. "You've got us now, okay? I've been having a lot of fun getting to know you."

Stevie's eyes shine. "Me too! I'm sorry I wasn't always nice to you."

I could brush off her apology with acceptance, but instead I take my hand away and ask, "Why weren't you?"

She doesn't seem fazed by the question. I've learned that Stevie appreciates people who are up front with her, even if she doesn't always trust it because of Tessa. While she mulls over her answer, I slip off my shoes and play with the sand, squishing it between my toes.

"I don't know. You think you're a good person, and then someone like Tessa comes into your life. She has a way of making you believe—or want to believe—that you really *are* better than everyone else." Stevie presses her lips together for a moment. "But some part of you knows it's wrong. You get so caught up in it that you don't know how to stop. You feel like you deserve it because . . . because there are all sorts of tests you have to pass to keep your spot in Tessa's circle. It feels good when you pass them. And it's a weird sense of power. It's sort of addicting, even if it isn't right."

I kick my pile of sand, destroying it before I respond. "That sounds really complicated and not fun at all."

"It wasn't." Stevie takes a deep breath. "Sometimes when Dallas tells me something, like how he's happy I'm around, I expect it to be a test—like I have to prove that I'm worthy enough for you—but then you'll say the same thing, and it makes me realize you're really just friends who like me."

"You haven't given us a reason not to."

Stevie's face is filled with worry. "I don't want to. Ever."

"I believe you." I feel as though I'll have to reassure her of that a lot. "Think you'll join soccer again?"

"Maybe," Stevie murmurs. "It's too late for the fall soccer team, but I can always join in spring. I actually miss it."

"Then why'd you stop playing . . . ?" I let my voice trail off. I know the answer.

"Um. Tessa didn't think it was a good idea," Stevie murmurs. Her voice is so soft. I don't really know what to do when she gets like this, but I want to wrap a blanket around her and shield her from the world.

We make our way over to the jungle gym and climb into it, settling on the metal floor. Stevie idly plays with the fake steering wheel above her head, and it creaks as if it needs some oil. It's the only noise in the park.

I stretch my legs out and take a deep breath. This moment feels right.

"I'm nonbinary."

Stevie drops her hand from the steering wheel to look at me with wide eyes. "Cool. They/them, then?"

I smile and nod. "Yeah."

"Is that why you go by Jude now too?"

"Yep." I lean back on the palms of my hands. "I know it's not shocking or anything but . . ."

"Thanks for telling me," Stevie is quick to say. She smiles. "You didn't have to tell me, you know. I would've still called you Jude and used they/them pronouns for you. I noticed Dallas never genders you, so . . . I guess I kind of knew. But you didn't have to tell me."

My heart fills, and my voice cracks. "Th-thank you."

"I'm glad you did, though." Stevie lets out a breath, and I wonder if she's about to come out to me. Instead, she asks, "What's the best part about being nonbinary?"

The question takes me by surprise, and I turn it over in my head. Stevie doesn't seem bothered by the silence, so I tuck my legs in, then cross and uncross them a few times. The way Stevie looks at me . . . it's clear that she *cares*. She wants to know. She's ready and listening.

"The relief I felt when I had a word for it," I say. My voice is soft like Stevie's was. "Realizing that neither binary gender fits me. I'm not a boy. I'm not a girl. I just . . . *am*. And that's okay. I don't have to fit into some box. Plus, nonbinary can be an identifying label in itself *and* an umbrella term for anything outside the male-female binary."

Stevie shakes her head. "I didn't know that. So, how do you use it?"

"It's a label for me. It makes me feel good. Safe. Like I'm not alone, y'know?" I give her a quick smile. "Knowing there's a community of people who feel the same messy way about gender out there . . ."

"It matters," Stevie says, with a knowing nod, "to know that nothing's wrong with you."

I laugh. It's not funny, but Stevie gets it, and that's all I care about right now. "Yes, exactly. Once I figured out I wasn't cis, this massive weight lifted off me. It was like I wasn't lying anymore. I can be me, and that's okay."

"When did you figure it out?"

"When Demi Lovato came out as nonbinary and told the world their pronouns are they/them. I didn't know exactly what it meant, so I googled. And it just felt like coming home."

Stevie shivers and pulls her hood up. It's not that cold out, but she looks cute tucked into Dallas's dark blue hoodie, her blond hair popping out the sides. She shoves her hands into the front pocket. "Thanks for telling me, Jude."

"Thanks for being someone I could tell," I reply. We share a smile and a silent moment. Nothing else needs to be said right now.

A small sense of peace washes over me and settles deep into my chest. *Someone else knows who I am. I don't have to pretend to be anyone else with Stevie.* I tilt my head back and look up at the roof of the jungle gym. It's covered in graffiti—from both spray paint and Sharpies.

"Hey, I have an idea." I reach into my backpack and pull out my pencil case. Whipping out a Sharpie, I hold it up proudly. "Want to vandalize?"

"Oh my god." Stevie laughs. "Sure. For the record, if it wasn't already covered in marker, I would say no. But when something's already full of graffiti, you might as well make your own mark. What do you want to write?"

"Hmm," I say, playing with the marker in my hand. "I don't know. We could just sign our names?"

"Boring. But I don't have a better idea, so . . ." Stevie

stands up and nudges me. "We should write the date, though. Today was an important day."

I smile at her. "Okay. Thanks for, you know, making this a safe space and all."

Stevie's eyes flash with excitement. She snatches the Sharpie from my hand and walks around until she settles on a small patch close to the lip of the roof; then she says, "Let's do it here. Sign your name."

I write *Jude* beside her *Stevie*. She takes the Sharpie back to add some little hearts and the date. Above the year, she writes *OUR SAFE SPACE* and then draws a box around it.

She looks at me, her face bright. I laugh because everything feels right.

Then I quietly say, "For the record, I'm bisexual too."

"Yeah?"

"Yeah."

"All right." Stevie opens her arms and wraps me in a tight hug. "You're pretty freaking cool, Jude."

I don't actually know how to respond to that, but it doesn't matter.

Stevie doesn't come out in turn, and I'm not bothered by it. That should never have been my reason for coming out to her. Dallas was right; it should have always been me just wanting to tell her who I am.

A wave of lightness hits me, and I try to memorize the feeling. I don't know when I'll experience it again, or even if I ever will.

"Want to go on the seesaw?"

"Yes!" I shout, darting past her in an unspoken race to get there first. Stevie shouts after me, but she's running, and soon we're laughing and arguing about who got there first.

And you know what?

I think it was probably as close to a perfect coming out as I'll ever get.

CHAPTER 11

"Do you need anything?" Dallas asks Aspen for the second time since we all got off the bus. Our plan is to make friendship bracelets upstairs in Dallas's room while she watches TV down here. Since his dad is away for business, there's no chance of us having to sneak out later.

Aspen turns to look at us over her shoulder. "Do I ever need anything from you?"

Dallas shrugs, but Stevie gives her a bright smile. I know that look—she means business. Stevie says, "No, but you'd miss it if he stopped asking. What are you going to watch?"

"*High School Musical: The Musical: The Series,*" Aspen answers, shrugging. Her shrugs are so identical to Dallas's that it's almost funny. It's just one of those sibling traits, I guess. Aspen pulls at her ear, a habit that only started once Stevie came around. "Season four just released, and it's really good so far."

"I love that show!" Stevie says. "The characters are all amazing."

"And funny," Aspen says, a smile starting to spread on her

lips. "The first season is still my favorite. I've seen it so many times. It was so good."

"It was," Stevie agrees.

"I'm going to make you a snack," Dallas announces before rushing into the kitchen.

"I don't need a snack!" Aspen shouts after him, but we all know it's fruitless.

"What about *Eden Jones?*" Stevie asks, settling into the chair beside the couch. "Have you seen that one?"

Aspen hesitates before admitting, "No."

"Oh! You'd absolutely love it. It's about a kid who lies to their mom about having friends," Stevie says. "So the whole show is about how they get all these other kids to pretend to be their friends for a birthday party. The season leads up to the party but ends on a cliff-hanger."

"What's the cliff-hanger?" Aspen leans in, as if she can't help herself.

"I don't want to spoil it for you."

"You can," Aspen says, nodding. "It's all about the journey anyway."

"That's how I feel too!" Stevie exclaims.

"So?"

"Okay, well, the whole season leads up to the party, and the doorbell rings, but then it ends! We don't know who's at the door, or if it's even one of their fake friends. Someone on Twitter thought it could be the pizza delivery person." Stevie's hands fly around, and she shifts to the edge of the chair cushion. "We have to wait until December to find out what happens."

"Oh my god," Aspen says. "That's torture. I haven't even seen it, and I want to know."

"Exactly. You should check it out."

"I will," Aspen says, casually stealing glances at Stevie. Then she calls over her shoulder, "Hey, butthead! Where are my snacks?"

Dallas comes out of the kitchen, shaking his head in amusement as he brings Aspen a plate of carrots, cucumber, and celery with peanut butter on it. "I thought you didn't want any."

Aspen sticks her tongue out at him.

"Okay," I say, and everyone glances at me as if they'd forgotten I was there. "Can we go upstairs now?"

"Rude," Aspen says, but I know she hardly means it.

"Yes," Dallas answers, nudging his sister. "Yell if you need anything, and don't open the door to anyone."

"Yeah, yeah. I know the drill," Aspen says.

Once we're in Dallas's room, we settle down on the floor and Stevie pulls out her friendship bracelet kit.

"You haven't opened it yet?" I ask, spreading the colored threads out on the floor while Stevie unfolds the instructions and Dallas picks up the plastic thread holder that comes with the kit. "I thought you said your mom got it for you last year."

"Um, yeah, she did." Stevie looks up from the instructions. "But Tessa thought it was dumb."

"Oh."

"Yeah. But I kept the kit because I still wanted to make them. There are all these different patterns you can do, and you can add beads to it if you want."

"I don't know if I'm quite up to that yet. I've never made one of these before," I admit.

We spend the next twenty minutes picking out our threads—I choose pink, purple, and blue for Stevie's bracelet; Dallas chooses yellow, orange, and red for mine; and Stevie chooses rainbow threads for Dallas's. It takes us another ten to figure out how to even do the patterns. I pin my threads to my leggings with a little safety pin.

"I think I've got this," I say once I find a comfortable rhythm.

"You do!" Stevie grins. "Look at you go."

"Why did you use so much orange for me?" I ask, looking at Dallas. "It looks very citrusy."

"Because that's your favorite color."

"No, it isn't."

"Yes, it is."

"No."

"Yes."

"No, it isn't," I insist.

Stevie laughs. I glance at her. "What?" she says. "I just think it's funny that Dallas knows you better than you know you. You always choose orange over every other color. And you wear a lot of it too. It looks good on you; don't worry."

"Do I really?" I ask, looking down at my rusty-orange sweater. It's probably my second favorite after my red plaid shirt. I laugh. "Okay, well, this is just bad timing."

We all burst into giggles and then fall into an easy silence for a while, focusing on our bracelets.

It's only when I realize Stevie's sniffs are from tears that I look up.

"Stevie?"

"Sorry," she whispers, wiping at her eyes. "Sorry. I just . . . I never thought I'd get to do this with anyone."

I place my hand on her knee. "What do you mean?"

"After Tessa called my kit dumb, I . . ." Stevie takes a deep breath. "I guess I just thought I wouldn't be able to have friends who I could do stuff like this with."

"She made you feel like you'd never have any friends without her, didn't she?" I can't picture being friends with anyone like that, but then again, I've always had Dallas by my side.

"Yes."

"I'm sorry," Dallas says, frowning. "That really sucks."

"She just . . . She doesn't trust anyone. She thinks that friendship is a game. And she would get me to do all these really bad things. Like, once, I had to call Jacob Weeks and tell him I had a crush on him, even though I didn't!" Stevie says, tears falling down her cheeks. She swipes them away quickly. "And then I had to call him back and tell him I was just joking. It was so mean."

"So, then why did you do it?" Dallas asks.

"It's . . . It's hard to explain. You just get stuck in this . . ." Stevie takes a deep breath, but it's shaky, and I can tell she doesn't want to continue. "Vicious cycle."

"Hey, hey, it's okay. You don't have to talk about it anymore," I tell her, promising her with my eyes that we'll never make her do anything like that. She puts her hand on mine and squeezes.

"Thanks. I guess I'm still upset about it."

"Of course. Besides, I'm sure Jacob would forgive you if he knew you were pressured into it."

"Maybe." Stevie sighs. "Thanks."

"Of course!" Dallas says, nudging Stevie slightly. "Friends for life."

"Yeah."

We all share a silent smile and then turn back to focusing on our bracelets. When they're finished, we exchange them, putting them on one another's wrists. They aren't perfect. In fact, Dallas messed his up in two places. But they're beautiful and they mean the entire world to me.

CHAPTER 12

"Truth or dare?" I say to Stevie later that night. I'm so glad it isn't my turn again. I just finished drinking pickle juice from Dallas's fridge. I take another chug of my water, trying to wash down the taste, but it doesn't help.

Stevie giggles. "Truth."

"Okay." I pause, thinking about what I could possibly ask Stevie. There are a bunch of questions I still have, but I don't dare ask her any of them. Questions like *Are you queer? Is Tessa really not your friend anymore because you have a crush on a girl? How terrible is it to be friends with someone like Tessa?*

I rub my hand back and forth along the outside seam of my leggings as I try to think. Then I clap my hands together. Dallas leans in, excited.

"What's the best part of hanging out with us?"

"That's your truth question? Okay." Stevie looks at us. She lowers her head briefly, as if she has to think of the answer, then nods slightly while a grin spreads across her face. "I think the best part about hanging out with you both is how easy it is. There aren't any expectations. I can just be myself."

"Good answer," Dallas says approvingly. His eyebrows flash upward. "For the record, there is no wrong answer."

"Gee, thanks, Dal," Stevie says.

"Okay, so it's Stevie's turn to say truth or dare," I say.

"Dallas, truth or dare."

"Hmm, truth," he says.

"Have you ever had feelings for Jude? Like romantic ones?" Stevie asks, wiggling her eyebrows.

I scrunch my nose up immediately. *Oh no.* We're not even safe from Stevie! For as long as I can remember, everyone has been cracking jokes that Dallas and I would end up falling in love. *Ew.* No offense to Dallas. He's an amazing person, and he's my person, the one I want by my side no matter what. But he's not *that* person to me.

Dallas refuses to look at me, instead pulling his collar up to cover his mouth and nose. "Ew, Stevie. Jude is just my best friend. Am I not allowed to be close with someone without being asked if we're gonna fall in love and kiss?"

"Ew," I say, grabbing a pillow from the bed and smacking Dallas. "Don't even say those words."

Dallas starts laughing, and I can't help but join in. We both look at Stevie expectantly, and she's trying to hide her smile. "I wasn't serious," she says. "I'm just teasing!"

"Had me fooled," Dallas grumbles. He tosses the pillow

at Stevie, who catches it. "What's your real question?"

"Do you have a crush on anyone?"

I'm curious to know the answer to this. I scoot forward on the floor, cupping my chin with my hands, and give Dallas a look. We don't really talk about romantic things, mostly because it's not been a major interest to us before.

Dallas shakes his head. "No, I don't."

"Hmm, is he lying?" Stevie stage-whispers to me.

I eye Dallas, then shake my head. "Nah, he's being honest."

There *was* that one guy, but I'm not about to out my best friend. I shift and then Dallas surprises me by saying, "I have had a crush before, though."

"Ooh, who?" Stevie asks.

"Um," Dallas starts, then looks at me. "Jude, can you . . . ?"

"No, no," I say, shaking my head. I reach out and put my hand on his knee. "This is yours to share."

"I'm gay," Dallas murmurs.

Stevie glances at me before she smiles. "Thanks for sharing that with me, Dal."

He looks up, mouth falling open. Then he snaps it shut and nods.

"So, there was this guy," I say, grinning.

"Jude!" Dallas hisses.

"It's just Stevie." I turn to her and say, "He had the biggest crush on this guy, Rowan McKinnon, from space camp last year. Rowan lives in the city, but for that entire week, Dallas was *all* about Rowan."

"I suppose since you're one of us now, you can hear about Rowan. He was really funny," Dallas adds.

Stevie gives Dallas a bright smile. "I like knowing things about you two."

"What about you?" Dallas asks, looking at Stevie. I smack his leg, and he flinches. "What? Oh. Sorry."

"It's not her turn." *And also, Stevie isn't out to us.* I try to communicate with him silently. He rubs the spot where I smacked him while Stevie gives me a grateful smile.

"Sorry, sheesh. Okay, Jude, truth or dare?" Dallas asks, smirking. "C'mon, don't be scared."

"I just drank pickle juice!"

Dallas giggles, and I swear, it's hard to be outraged when he does that. I start laughing, Stevie starts laughing, and the three of us dissolve into laughter.

"You really did," Dallas says, nodding. "How gross was it?"

"So gross," I say, and Stevie hands the pillow to me. I smack Dallas. "Dare. I'm not afraid of nothing."

"Hmm," Dallas says, stroking his invisible beard. I roll my eyes and give the pillow back to Stevie. She tosses it onto the bed behind her. "What if I dare you to call someone?"

"Seems harmless enough," I say, nodding. "Okay. Should I just dial a random number?"

"What if you prank call . . . Tessa?"

"Um." I glance at Stevie; it takes me a second to read her expression. I'm not entirely sure what to say right away, but then I shake my head. "No. Truth, Dallas."

"What?" Dallas pouts. "Are you chicken?"

"No, just—"

I shake my head again and move my eyes from him to Stevie. Maybe prank calling Tessa is something we would've done without Stevie in our group, but now that she's here, it doesn't seem as fun.

"You should do it," Stevie says. "Payback for all the times she made me prank call someone."

Dallas and I look at each other. Then I hold out my hand. "All right, give me your phone."

"What? Why mine?" Dallas asks.

"I had to give Tessa my phone number last year when we were forced to work on that English project, and she'll definitely have Stevie's number still."

"Ugh, fine." Dallas hands over his phone.

"What's her number?" I ask Stevie. She pulls out her phone and reads it off as I type. I grimace as I put it on speaker phone.

"Hello?" Tessa answers after a moment.

"Is your fridge running?" I blurt, unable to think of anything else. We should've talked this through.

"What?"

"Well, you better go catch it!" I say the punch line anyway. I smack a hand to my face as Dallas and Stevie muffle their laughter.

"Wait—*Jude*?"

I cringe at the sound of my deadname, and Dallas immediately reaches over to put his hand on my knee.

"Oh, *sorry*, I guess it's Jude now, isn't it?" Tessa continues without sounding sorry at all. "Whatever. Don't you or your loser *friend* call me again. How childish are you?"

I want to tell her that Dallas isn't a loser, want to rub it in her face that we're friends with Stevie now, want to point out that she made Stevie do this before, but instead I find myself frozen.

"Tessa," Stevie says in a warning tone. "Don't be hurtful."

"Stevie?" Tessa asks, sounding a little smaller. It occurs to me that Tessa might actually *miss* Stevie. I know I would.

Stevie reaches over and hangs up the phone for me.

"Jude? You okay?" she asks quietly.

I plaster a smile on my face. "Yeah," I say, but I'm not sure either of them believes me.

"How about we ask Jude if they have a crush on anyone?" Stevie asks, changing the subject swiftly.

I blink. It's such an easy question. "Nope. No one for me."

"Not even someone like Shelby?"

"She's cute, but not my type."

"What is your type?" Stevie asks, shifting on her butt. She stretches out a leg.

"I'm not sure," I answer honestly. "But I know I'm queer. I think about the idea of dating someone nonbinary like me, or maybe holding hands with a girl, or even kissing a boy. I can picture myself with anyone, really. I think I'd prefer to be with a girl, or someone who is nonbinary. Boys are too . . . um."

"Dirty, rude, annoying?" Stevie suggests.

I snap my fingers. "Yes, that."

"How do you think I feel?" Dallas says, dramatically throwing his hands into the air. "I mean, I'm not into girls. Or Jude. I'm just gay. And there are zero cute boys at our school. I remember when Howie ate worms in kindergarten. I think I'm good," Dallas says, shaking his head.

"Maybe when we're older?" Stevie suggests.

"I hope so," I say, shrugging. "I'd be okay with being single forever, though. Me and my six cats. Sounds nice."

We all start laughing.

"Truth or dare, Stevie."

"Truth," she says, covering her face and peeking out between her fingers. "I don't want to drink pickle juice!"

I laugh. "Okay, what's something you've never told anyone?"

"Um." Stevie takes a breath. "Okay, but you can't tell *anyone* this."

I'm sure it's happening. Stevie is going to come out to us, and we're all finally going to be able to talk about it!

"What's up?" Dallas asks, leaning forward.

"My dad's girlfriend is a horse girl, right? Like, she *loves* horses. She grew up on a farm. And she keeps buying me all this horse-related stuff." Stevie takes a deep breath. I share a questioning look with Dallas. "She got me a horse wallet, a horse blanket, a horse figure . . . Every gift is a horse."

"Okay . . . ?" I say.

"And I hate horses. I'm *terrified* of them."

I start to giggle. "WHAT?"

"They're so big! One kick from a horse and you could *die*. They could *throw* you off them. And, like—" Stevie stops talking. "Quit laughing!"

But we can't. I say, "THIS is what you haven't told anyone? Your big secret?"

"Yes! My dad thinks it's great that I'm bonding with

his girlfriend. I don't have the heart to tell them."

Dallas wheezes. "Oh my god, that's so funny."

"How many gifts has she given you?" I ask.

"At least twelve."

Dallas and I giggle again, and Stevie starts to join us.

"Swear you'll never tell," she says. Dallas and I immediately offer up our pinkie fingers.

It's one of those nights I want to cling to forever. Everything is going right; everything feels right.

• • •

We eat leftover lasagna for dinner, then decide on a movie. By the end of *Love Potioned*, Stevie's already asleep. I'm almost certain she's drooling.

I look at Stevie sleeping and smile; things have been really good since I came out to her. The other day, she even sent me nonbinary icon Halsey's new song and a gay meme that made me laugh. I can't stop thinking about how she wrote *OUR SAFE SPACE* on the playground equipment. Sometimes, it feels like safe spaces are hard to find—a place where anyone can be themselves fully and not judged for it.

I wonder if others are looking for their safe spaces.

Dallas pokes my arm and then waves his hand in front of me. I try to keep my face straight, but it's next to impossible when he gives me the sassiest expression back.

I crack first, and Dallas cheers, throwing a fist into the air. "Crushed it."

I roll my eyes. "What?"

"You're a little quieter than usual right now. Everything okay? I know it's been a long day, but . . ." Dallas looks concerned. "You've been more wrapped up in your thoughts lately. What's up, Jude?"

"Oh!" I swallow because I'm not sure what to say. "I guess I've just been . . . Well, I was thinking about how I came out to Stevie, actually."

"Oh yeah?"

"It's just . . . I don't really know why I said it, but when Stevie thanked me for coming out to her, I thanked her for being a safe space."

"This makes sense now—I saw your thing in the jungle gym."

"You did?"

"Well, Aspen did." Dallas shrugs. "Hope it's okay that I added my name above yours. But there's space, so people won't really know we're connected. I didn't want to overstep on your thing with Stevie."

"Oh my god, of course!" I laugh. "Stevie will be happy you did, I bet."

"Anyway, so you thanked Stevie for being a safe space?"

95

"Right." I nod and shift on the bed. "I keep thinking of that phrase."

"Safe space?"

"Yeah." I fiddle with the corner of the comforter. I sigh heavily and scrunch my nose, just like Dallas does. "We don't really have anything like that here."

"You mean in school?"

"Well, yeah, but also Aberdeen Falls in general." I wave my hand around. "At least, I've never seen anything advertised."

Dallas gives me a look, and I know he's already thinking what I'm thinking. He nudges me with his foot and wiggles his eyebrows. "All right, Jude, so what are we going to do about it?"

• • •

The following Wednesday, the three of us are hanging out at Dallas's again when we hear the door slam downstairs. Stevie says, "Hey, Jude, want to walk with me to the park?"

"Sure. Catch you later, Dal?" I ask.

"Sounds good."

Stevie stops to say goodbye to Aspen by messing up her hair, then we slip out the side door. She jogs to fall into step with me.

"That's always awkward."

"Yeah." I shrug. It's kind of sad that it's almost normal now.

We don't talk much, both lost in our own thoughts as we walk to the playground. There are a couple of teenagers on the swings, but they're gone by the time we've climbed up the jungle gym. I guess they don't want to hang around in the same place as a couple of kids.

"Hey, I packed some nail polish. I was hoping we could do each other's nails," Stevie says, squirming a little. "What do you say?"

"Sure," I answer. "What colors do you have?"

"I couldn't pack all of them, but . . ." Stevie reaches into her bag, feeling around for her pouch. She unzips it and pulls out a rusty orange. "I brought your favorite color."

I laugh.

"Don't tell Dallas," I say with an attempt at a wink, "but I love it."

"I knew it!"

We giggle, and I let Stevie paint my nails. "Did Tessa teach you this?"

"Yep." Stevie frowns. "It's weird. Before Tessa, I didn't have anyone to show me this kind of stuff. Soccer girls are different. They don't mind getting dirty, or even a little violent for that matter. They're tough and hard. But with Tessa, she was all . . ."

I don't push her to finish. I get it, sort of.

"Tessa was all sparkles and unicorns and girly things. It's weird," Stevie eventually continues. "Because you and Dallas are sort of like the middle ground. I like it much better."

"I'm glad."

She lifts her head. "All done!"

"What?" I look down at my nails, and sure enough, they're rusty orange. I grin. "Why do you even have this color? It doesn't seem very Tessa-like."

"It's not. She'd lose her mind if she knew I bought it. But I picked it up for you. Figured you'd come around to your love of orange eventually."

I laugh. "Yeah, okay. But I don't like when Dallas is right too often. It goes to his head."

Stevie snorts. "I could see that. So, what do you think?"

"They're perfect."

And they are. My attempt at Stevie's nails is almost laughable, but she's calm as she directs me on how to do it. She brought tissue to keep things clean and gets me to touch up a couple bits on her skin. Overall, it's not the best job, but it doesn't look that bad. Stevie admires her hands.

"They're perfect," she says.

"They're awful."

"They're done with love, so they're perfect." Just like the friendship bracelets.

I don't say anything to that, just watch Stevie admire her nails. A small smile grows on my face, and I can't stop the contented sigh that whooshes out of me. My body feels all loose, and I wonder if it can always be like this.

Stevie slipped into my world and changed it forever.

And I'm so glad she did.

CHAPTER 13

"It's weird," I say, climbing onto Stevie's bus with Dallas. "I've never been on a bus that wasn't Mei's before. Like, other than for school trips."

"Huh, now that you say it, neither have I!" Dallas replies.

I shoot him a *duh!* look, and he grins. Stevie waves us over, and we settle into a row near the back of the bus. Dallas sits with Stevie, and I get my own seat. We pile up our backpacks beside me so Dallas and Stevie have more room.

"Do you like your bus driver?" I ask after a while, keeping my voice low.

Stevie shrugs. "Sure, I guess. I've had a couple of drivers, but none were nice like Mei."

"Huh," Dallas says, craning his neck to look out the window. "I don't think I've really been to this part of town much."

"Me neither. Except there's an awesome—" I start.

"Ice cream store—" Dallas continues.

"On Haggett Street!" Stevie finishes.

We all beam. Then Stevie tells us the best news: "I live right beside it, and the soccer field I love isn't far from it either."

"Okay, we're *so* getting ice cream tonight," I say. I reach across the aisle and playfully poke Dallas. "Don't let me get too hyper on sugar."

"Ha. As if I could ever control you," Dallas says, snorting. "Jude, you're going to do whatever you want to do."

"True."

"What's your favorite ice cream?" Stevie asks.

We're still arguing about the best ice cream flavor by the time we get off at Stevie's stop and head to Haggett's Scoops. Stevie holds the door as Dallas and I trip over each other to get inside.

"Okay, okay," Stevie says. "I see you two are serious about your ice cream."

"Very," Dallas says so drily that even I don't know if he's kidding.

We quickly order and make our way down the road to the soccer fields. Sitting in a circle near one of the nets, we eat our ice cream. When I finish, I lean back on the palms of my hands and look around. I picture Stevie playing a game on these fields, scoring a goal. The crowd goes wild, and she comes running toward Dallas and me on the sidelines.

"What's special about this field?" I ask, looking across to the other net.

Stevie shrugs. "Nothing, really. But I sort of fell in love

with soccer here . . . I brought my ball in case you wanted to play a little two-on-one."

"I like those odds," Dallas says.

"I don't!" I protest. But then I break into a big smile. "You're on!"

I hop onto my feet and tug the soccer ball out of Stevie's tote bag. I drop it in front of me and start kicking it toward the goal. I glance back to see Dallas moving our bags off the field and Stevie hot on my heels.

I squeal when she kicks the ball away from me and into her possession. Slowing to a stop, I watch as she powers her way down the field and shoots into the open net. She throws her hands in the air and shouts, "Woo-hoo! Morgan scores the winning goal!"

"The crowd goes wild!" I yell, cheering her on as she jogs back toward us.

Dallas runs up to my side and whistles with his fingers between his lips.

Stevie laughs, and I think it's the first time I've seen her be truly free. I love every moment of it. Then Dallas says, "C'mon, Morgan. Get the ball, and let's get this game started!"

"I'm still going to kick your butts!" Stevie shouts as she barrels toward us with the ball, doing fancy kicks down the length of the field.

Dallas is clearly impressed by Stevie's skills.

Stevie dances around me before darting past with the ball.

"You're like a soccer pro!" I call out while chasing her. I'm out of breath by the time she scores.

"Man, that feels good," Stevie says before passing the ball to me. "It's been a *long* time since I kicked a ball around outside of gym class."

"I bet," I say. Then I call over to Dallas, "Try to headbutt it!"

I take the ball to the edge of the field and throw it to Dallas. He heads it toward our net.

"Go, Dallas!" Stevie calls out.

"This is a lot harder than it looks," Dallas says, jogging beside me. Stevie gets to the ball first and swipes it back toward her net.

"She's *good*," I comment.

"Yeah. Sucks that she had to drop soccer."

I glance at Dallas and nod. It *does* suck that she had to drop soccer. I hate that Tessa took this from her.

Stevie wipes out, getting a huge grass stain on her leggings, but she just tosses her head back and soaks up the sun's rays. I steal the ball while she's having a moment, then pass it to Dallas. Stevie launches herself onto her feet and runs past me. But it's too late—Dallas scores.

I scream, and Dallas and I high-five. Stevie pants and says, "Great work."

"Thanks for inviting us," I say. "Soccer's not so bad."

Stevie half laughs as Dallas claps me on the shoulder.

• • •

It's a Friday when Stevie pulls something out of her backpack at the park.

I'm swinging while Dallas kicks the dirt with his shoes. He didn't have to babysit Aspen today, because she's gone to a friend's for a sleepover; it's like he almost doesn't know what to do with his free time.

"Whatcha got?" I ask Stevie, craning my neck to see.

"Jude, close your eyes! I have a surprise for you."

I do, and then she laughs and tells me to stop swinging for a minute. It takes me a moment to stop, but I do. Maybe she has something for me, or maybe she's going to throw a pie in my face. I don't know, and I don't care. I'm ready to be surprised.

"Hold out your hands."

She places something in them, something soft.

"Okay, open them."

I look down, and the grin that hits my face is unstoppable. "Oh my god!"

"It's a progress pride flag!"

"I love it. This is for me?" I ask, unfolding it. It's

massive—the perfect size to be a cape. I immediately want to wrap myself in it and never let it go. It's beautiful, and no one's ever bought me a pride thing before. Once, I asked Mom for a rainbow shirt, and she looked at the price and said it was too expensive. I didn't ask again after that.

"It is. I saw it at the dollar store and asked my mom if we could pick it up for you. She said yes, and . . . yeah. Do you like it?"

"I love it!"

"I want one!" Dallas says, a whine in his voice.

"Lucky for you," Stevie says, going back to her backpack again, "I got one for each of us. Maybe we could go to Pride together, sometime."

"Thanks, Stevie," Dallas says, grinning.

I tie mine around my neck, hop off the swing, and run around. "Woo! I'm a nonbinary superhero!"

"I'm in!" Dallas shouts, and then he gets Stevie to help him tie his flag around his neck.

The three of us run around the park with our pride-flag capes, pretending to protect those who cannot protect themselves, solving imaginary crimes, and fighting invisible villains. It's the happiest I've been in a long, long time. In fact, I can't remember ever being this happy before.

• • •

We walk over to my house for dinner, and Stevie heads home afterward. Dallas stays for a classic Friday-night sleepover complete with gummy worms and movies. Before we get ready for bed, he helps me hang the pride flag on my bedroom wall.

"Hey, can we sleep in the same bed tonight?" Dallas asks. "I didn't feel like dragging your body pillow over, and I really don't want to crash on your couch."

"The windows?"

"The windows. It's too dark. Someone could be staring at you and you'd never know." Dallas shudders. "But I'll do it if you want. I don't want to make you uncomfortable or—"

I lift my hand up, but I don't speak. I'm trying to quickly gather my thoughts. We stopped sharing a bed after we came out to each other, and we never really talked about it. It seemed like the thing to do, I guess. But do I care if I sleep beside Dallas? It's not as if he's going to kiss me. (Ew.) It's just sleeping.

Dallas sarcastically twiddles his thumbs, but I know he's acting like a brat because of my pause. And he knows I have to take time to sort out my thoughts. It's not easy to think on the spot for me like it is for him.

"I'm okay with it," I decide.

"Absolute?" he asks.

"Absolute," I reply with a firm nod. Then I yawn. "Is it bedtime already?"

"Yes."

It doesn't take long before we're both snuggled into my bed. There's space between us, but not so much that we're falling off the edges. I yawn again and roll over to face him.

"Thanks for letting me sleep over," Dallas whispers.

"Do you want to talk or be distracted?" I ask, knowing where this will lead.

"I think I want to talk," Dallas decides. His voice is filled with hesitation when he starts talking again. "I think my parents should get a divorce."

I reach out so I can grab his hand. He intertwines his fingers in mine and squeezes tight. I can see the tears building in his eyes. "I'm sorry, Dallas. But that's probably for the best."

"I know," Dallas whispers. The tears slip over the bridge of his nose, down his cheek, and onto his pillow. "But I don't understand why they can't work it out."

"What are they even fighting about?"

"Everything and *nothing*. Last night, my mom started shouting that my dad had parked in her spot. I didn't even know she *had* a parking spot until they were yelling at each other." Dallas swallows hard. "Stevie was over. I couldn't get her out in time."

"Oh no. How did she react?"

"She hugged me." Dallas squeezes his eyes shut. "Do you think that people are doomed to never find love?"

"What?! Dallas, how could you even think that? We're only twelve. We have our whole lives ahead of us!"

"I know, but . . . your mom's single. My parents can't make it work. Stevie's parents are divorced . . ." Dallas sighs, brushing his eyes with his hand. "The future looks bleak for us, Jude. Don't you think?"

I shift my head, but I can't look at Dallas right now. I stare at the dark ceiling. "Honestly, when you put it like that . . ."

"Yeah."

"But I don't want to live in a world where our future looks bleak. Do you?" I ask, unsure if I'm asking Dallas or myself.

He swallows before answering. "Guess not."

"Then let's live in a world filled with hope and love," I decide.

"Okay," Dallas whispers back. "Jude?"

"Yeah?"

"Do you think Stevie's parents fought as much as mine before their divorce?"

"I don't know. You're pulling out all the hard questions tonight, huh?" I fiddle with the corner of my comforter.

"That's what I'm here for," Dallas tells me. He yawns, shifting as though he's uncomfortable with the conversation.

"Now, if only I could solve my parents' marriage . . . or help them finally agree on a divorce."

"Oof," I murmur.

"Yeah."

We fall silent for so long, I almost think that Dallas has fallen asleep. But then he asks, "Do you think we're going to be okay? Sometimes, the universe feels like it's crushing me, and I don't know if I'm going to make it."

"We're going to be okay," I whisper, but I'm not entirely sure I believe it myself. I roll over to snuggle closer with him. He snuggles into me back, and I'm glad we're throwing the weird no-sharing-a-bed rule out the window. This is more comfortable, being close to each other for the sake of feeling close and nothing else.

"You really think so?" Dallas asks.

"I know so," I lie. But I'll take that lie to my grave before I let Dallas ever know I have no idea if we're going to be okay. I hate that he feels the weight of the world on his shoulders.

"Love you, Jude."

"Love you too, Dallas."

"Hey, Jude?"

"Yeah?"

"Have you thought any more about your safe-space idea?"

A smile crosses my face; I couldn't hide it if I tried. I

reach over to my bag and grab my journal, flipping it open to the page I had been working on earlier in English class. I show it to him in the moonlight. "I think it's time Aberdeen gets a safe space, don't you?"

He skims my list of ideas.

"I'm in," he says, grinning. "But you knew that already. Where are we going to start?"

"I'm hoping we can start with the school, but I'm worried that will limit it to just us. Plus, I checked, and Rose Creek doesn't have anything for marginalized communities either."

"Marginalized meaning People of Color? Because that'd be cool."

"Yeah! People of Color, queer people, and disabled folk," I explain. "I read about it in a book."

"Of course you did," Dallas says, shaking his head with a smile on his face. "Okay, so again, how do we start?"

"I'm not sure, to be honest. I figured we could go in and talk to the principal. They're usually good about stuff like that, right?" I pull my notebook closer and scan my list of things I want to do. They've been churning around in the back of my head for two weeks now—ever since the night I came out to Stevie. I finally had to write them down or I wouldn't be able to think about anything else.

110

"Maybe," Dallas says, shrugging. "I think having it open to both Rose Creek and Aberdeen Falls will be our best bet, so maybe we can ask the school about that. Who knows how many queer people are around, you know?"

"True. It's not like people are incredibly open about it here." I frown. I hate the idea of people being forced to hide. It seems so unfair. Then I remember my grandparents and how I have to hide myself from them, and my brow furrows. It *is* unfair.

"What are we going to call it?" Dallas asks in a whisper.

I frown, staring at the ceiling. "Um . . . Aber-Rose? Aber-Creek?"

"What about Rosedeen?" Dallas offers.

I roll my head to look at him. "It's perfect. Rosedeen Safe Space: where all marginalized people are welcome."

"Yeah. Thanks for thinking of People of Color," Dallas whispers. We don't talk about the color of his skin much, but I know he has experienced some vastly different challenges than I have.

I twist my shirt a little in my hand. "Of course. I know that they'll understand you in ways I never can."

Dallas looks at me. "And you'll always understand me in ways they never can."

"Heh. Thanks." I smile at him, and then an idea comes to

me. "How do we make sure that people from marginalized communities find out about us?"

"You're thinking ten steps ahead, but I think we could put up posters . . . ?"

We keep talking about ideas for the club until we're both yawning; then we decide we'd better go to sleep.

I close my eyes and listen to his breathing.

Eventually, it evens out, and I know he's asleep.

I roll away from him and snuggle against my pillow. Sleep doesn't come as easily to me—my mind races with possibilities, questions, concerns, and worries. I want Dallas to be okay, and I want to create a space that's safe for anyone.

CHAPTER 14

I can't let the idea of a safe space go. It keeps swirling around in my head, but I'm not entirely sure where to start. It seems a little too much for a twelve-year-old kid to handle, but whenever I find free time, my mind wanders.

I can see the possibilities. I can see it growing. There would be a few meetings a week for different age groups or different focuses. Like a support group, an activist group, and a friendly hang group. Queer people could find a space where they can just *be*. No questions asked. No judgment.

Everyone would share their experiences, their thoughts, their worries, and know that others get it. Not just understand it—actually *Get It*. It could be a place to share advice, jokes, life stories—even gender-affirming *clothes*.

Maybe it would lead to something bigger—a prouder, more open community in Aberdeen Falls and Rose Creek.

How many people are hiding? How many kids are like me but don't have the words? Who don't know that there are others like them? Who eat lunch alone, thinking that no one will ever accept them for who they are? How many people are living in survival mode, waiting for the day when they can move out of the Aberdeen Falls and Rose Creek area? Who is trapped here?

Who thinks they're alone?

Because before Dallas and I came out to each other, I thought I was.

"Where's your head at, kid?" Nan asks, leaning over to brush my cheek. I look up at her, wondering if she saw the article I left on her tablet. I've searched her face the last couple of Mondays, but I haven't found any answers.

Except this time she called me *kid*.

My eyes widen, and my lips part. I have no idea what I'm about to say, but Pops shatters the moment anyway. "Probably thinking about some trashy Netty show."

"You mean Netflix, Dad," my mom says, giving him a tired smile.

"They're not all trashy shows. Why don't you let me get you and Nan a profile? I think you'll change your tune if you give it a chance," I say.

"Bah. Who needs that? Kids like you need to get outside more. Sitting in front of a screen all day long, wasting away. It's ridiculous." Pops tsks and picks up his paper again. Without looking up, he calls out, "Betty! Clear the table."

I share a look with my mom. She's apologizing with her

eyes when an idea strikes me. I excuse myself from the dining table and sneak upstairs to my grandparents' bedroom. They have a TV in here, and just getting that to happen had taken Nan a lot of bargaining. While Nan wanted to watch late-night TV in bed, Pops would rather spend all evening in his recliner.

I don't understand my grandparents' relationship, but I know it's not what I want.

I create a new Netflix profile for my grandparents. I follow all the steps and then I leave the TV on. I search for my favorite queer shows and add them to my grandparents' list. If they never explore the unknown, how do they really know what they fear?

"**Jude**?" my grandmother says, deadnaming me, as she walks into the room.

Jude, I repeat in my head. *My name is Jude! Jude, Jude, Jude.* If I keep thinking about it, will she somehow know telepathically? If I keep pretending she's not deadnaming me, will she eventually stop?

"Your pops had a difficult day today. His friend was forced to retire early, and it's bringing a lot of insecurities out."

"Okay," I say, trying not to roll my eyes. I don't really care why Pops is grumpy tonight. He's almost always grumpy, rude, and unhelpful. I know he loves all of us, but it's hard to tell. He never expresses it. I can't remember the last time he told me he loved me—or, heck, even the last time we *hugged*.

Nan settles on the bed beside me and looks at the TV. She smiles, and it's warmer than usual. "Thank you . . ."

She doesn't repeat my deadname, and I can almost sense her biting her tongue. I fiddle with my hands in my lap and shrug. "Seems silly to hate Netflix. I'm sure he'll end up loving it. It's a bit overwhelming at first, and the algorithm needs work, but it's one of the easiest ways to watch things. I've even added some good shows to your list."

"Thank you. Pops has a tough time with change, you know. He can sometimes be stubborn, but—"

"Why do you make excuses for him?" I blurt. I'm not sure what makes me say that. It's something I've always wanted to know, but I've never had the guts to be so blunt.

Nan looks surprised, and I don't blame her. Usually, I'm quiet at our weekly dinners. That's starting to be harder, though. My emotions are right at the surface, just waiting to boil over.

"Is that what you think I do?"

"Don't you? Why isn't it Pops coming in here to say sorry for being rude?"

Yep. I can't stop now. My mouth has a mind of its own. I've

heard that saying before, but I'm finally experiencing it. It's a mix of exhilarating and terrifying.

Nan stares at me. I don't know what she's thinking. Her expression is as unreadable as always. She pats my hand and points to the screen. "Why don't you show me how to use this?"

"We're not going to talk about it?"

She shakes her head. "Not tonight, **Jude**."

I pretend she uses the right name.

• • •

"Jude, please. They're old," Mom says as she unlocks our front door.

"They're not *that* old," I point out, giving Mom a look. Her shoulders slump, and I don't blame her. If she acted like her parents did, I would be frustrated and deflated too. "Besides, I'm tired of seeing Pops treat Nan like she's his maid."

"He works hard—"

"And she doesn't?" I counter, crossing my arms. "Mom, I don't want to go back. Tonight sucked, but it sucks every Monday. Do *you* even like going?"

Mom makes a face, and I try not to laugh. The tension in the air slips away as she tosses an arm around my shoulders and pulls me close. "No, not really. I *suppose* I could take a hit for the team and get lunch with Nan on Friday. Just for this week, okay? Take a little breather from them, and we'll go back in two weeks. Let me call and talk to her."

"Thank you!" I shout, wrapping my arms around her waist. She holds me tight, kissing the top of my head.

"You know I'll always put you first, right?"

"Yeah." I smile up at her. "Thanks, Mom. I'm glad you're on my team."

"Back at you, kid." Mom pauses before quietly asking, "Does this also maybe have to do with you not being . . . out to them?"

"Yep." I pull away, but I put my hand on her arm so she knows I'm not upset with her. "It really sucks, and I feel like I'm on edge around them all the time."

"One day." Mom gives me a wink. "I'll talk to Nan about lunch. Why don't you go tell Dallas and Stevie the good news?"

I grin. "Love you!"

"Love you too!" she shouts as I dart up the stairs.

Within minutes, I've texted them about my week off from family dinner, and I'm met with lots of emojis and cheers.

But the moment is soured when I think of the people who have to deal with that *every day*. With hiding who they are, who they love, or even their name. Just like Dallas. Maybe even Stevie. How hard it must be. How confusing and awful

I felt before I knew, and how I wanted to *explode* when I figured it out.

How telling people makes me feel light and free.

How there are people in Aberdeen Falls and Rose Creek who can't feel that way.

Rosedeen Safe Space *has* to exist.

People need it.

I need it.

CHAPTER 15

"And that's why we need the Rosedeen Safe Space."

I finish my presentation with a bright smile and wait. Mrs. Bayley and the principal, Miss Johnson, give each other a look. I'm fairly sure they're impressed, and I flash Dallas a thumbs-up.

"That was a great presentation," Miss Johnson starts, and my chest fills with pride. I spent all week working on it with Dallas. Stevie said she was busy with family stuff, so we didn't spend much time with her. I've decided I want to surprise her with the brand-new club once it's ready.

"However, I don't think we'll be able to move forward with the club at this time," she continues, looking down at the papers in front of her. I can't read her expression. "Aberdeen Falls is much more conservative than Rose Creek, and I'm worried it's not the right fit for our school community."

I deflate. "You're letting me down easy."

"I think this is a brilliant idea," Miss Johnson adds, "but one people might not be ready for."

Dallas reaches over to give my hand a little squeeze. I nod

and close the laptop. "Right. Thank you for your time."

"It was wonderful," Mrs. Bayley says, smiling.

I force a smile. "Thanks, Mrs. B."

"Please don't give up entirely," Miss Johnson adds. "It's an uphill battle with these types of things. You'd be pitching to two different PTAs, and it's hard to get anything approved by them. Maybe you'll have better luck once you're in high school." Her smile is sympathetic, but it doesn't make me feel any better.

• • •

I spend most of English class trying to think of a solution. I doodle in my workbook as Mrs. Bayley talks and sometimes glance over at Stevie. She's idly twisting pieces of hair that have fallen out of her bun.

"You okay?" Stevie whispers.

I shrug, because I can't easily tell her about the disaster of a meeting—Stevie doesn't even know about the RSS yet.

"Are you coming to Taco Tuesday next week?" I whisper. She missed the last one for family reasons.

"Um," Stevie says, before shaking her head. "I don't think so, sorry."

I start to ask why not, but she goes back to twisting her hair and listening to Mrs. Bayley. I stare at her for a moment before returning to my doodles.

Maybe Dallas and I can brainstorm a new plan for the RSS later. I hope so, because we've been working on an English project all week, but I've been in planning mode for the safe space.

"Does anyone know why Shakespeare does this?" Mrs. Bayley asks the class. I have *no* idea what she's talking about. And then she says, "Jude?"

Crap.

"Um . . ."

"Mrs. Bayley," Tessa says, throwing her hand in the air. "I know."

"I asked Jude," Mrs. Bayley says, looking at me.

"I, um, I don't know," I admit. I glance at Stevie, and she shrugs.

"Please try to pay attention, Jude."

"Sorry," I mumble.

"*I* know," Tessa says again, waving her hand around. I slink down in my chair.

Of course, Mrs. Bayley asks to see me after class.

"Is this about the RSS?" I ask innocently once the bell rings.

She shakes her head. "Actually, I was wondering if you had finished the project this week. I've seen you working on things in class that aren't your assignment."

"Oh, um, no . . . I haven't." I swallow. How does she

know? I thought I was being really sly. I hug my books to my chest. "I'm sorry. It's hard for me to work when . . ."

"When?"

"There are just a lot of thoughts in my head. I've been working on it at home!" That's a lie, but I can't afford to tell the truth. The assignment is *so* dull that I can't even be bothered to bring it home.

Mrs. Bayley looks concerned but doesn't call me out. "Okay. Just as long as you hand it in on the deadline. And I would like to see you working on that in class, *not* the RSS."

"Okay."

But I already know I'm going to procrastinate until the last minute. It's how I work best.

"I also would like you to take the next recess to clean out and organize your messy desk," Mrs. Bayley adds. "Perhaps a cleaner workspace will help you focus better."

I nod. Sure. My messy desk is the problem. It's not like my brain isn't stuffed to the brim with RSS stuff or anything, or like being fixated and messy isn't part of my ADHD. Right. Okay. I take a deep breath because she believes it will help.

• • •

It takes me a week to think of the perfect solution for the Rosedeen Safe Space. I call Dallas immediately.

"What's up?" he says when he answers the phone. "I

don't have long to chat. Mom will be home soon with the groceries."

"The county library," I say instead of a greeting. I'm buzzing with excitement. "If we can hold the RSS at the county library, we bypass *so* many issues. No teachers, parents, or PTA votes. And best of all, *kids who want to attend can say they're going to the library*. No one will have to out themselves!"

It's a rush, a flurry, a fantastic idea. And it's what I need to keep from losing my mind. Mom's Friday lunch with Nan happened, but it didn't go over so well.

Plus, Stevie's been weirdly distant lately. She missed this week's Taco Tuesday because she said her dad and his girlfriend needed her at home *again*. It's hard to know if she's lying or not, but something in my gut says she wasn't telling the whole truth.

I wait for Dallas to react to my idea, and when he does, he lets out a small whistle. "Should've known you would figure something brilliant out."

"It is brilliant, isn't it?" I ask, grinning. I rock back and forth on my heels. "I'm going to ask Mei to drop me off at the library one day next week since we drive right by it. Can you come?"

"Um . . ." His hesitation speaks volumes.

"Is everything okay?"

"Not really."

"Is this why you were listening to Felix Sandman this morning?"

"Uh, yeah."

I should've known. Felix Sandman's song "Boys With Emotions" is Dallas's go-to when things get *really* bad. How did I miss it?

"I knew you were disappointed about the RSS, so I didn't want to add to it or anything. But . . . well, things aren't great right now." Dallas sighs, and his voice drops into a whisper. "It's bad, Jude."

I slump down into my chair and rub the back of my neck. "What can I do? What do you need?"

"I don't know," Dallas admits. "I don't know. But I don't think I can handle much more of it."

I don't know what that means. Is he going to break down? I cradle the phone in my hand and close my eyes. "I'm sorry, Dal. I'm so sorry. You can always come here if you need to, you know that, right?"

"Yeah. Yeah, I know." Dallas lets out a small exhale. "Do you think I could come over this weekend? It's always worse when they're both home."

"Of course. I'll ask my mom."

"Um," Dallas says. "Do you think maybe . . . ?"

I read his mind. "Does Aspen need to come with you? And Paris and Jersey?"

"Maybe."

It's the first time it's ever been so bad that he's taken me up on the offer.

"Okay," I say. "Okay. I'll figure it out."

Suddenly, nothing else seems as important.

CHAPTER 16

I walk into the kitchen, where my mom has a bunch of her real estate papers spread across the table. Her eyebrows are pulled together, and she looks ready to fight someone. This might not be the best time, but when is?

"Mom, I was wondering . . ." I pause, waiting for her to look up. Instantly, her face smooths out into a small smile.

"Hey, honey."

"Could I have a big sleepover this weekend?" I fidget with my hands. "Like, Dallas, and his sisters, and Stevie?"

"Dallas's sisters? That's unusual," she says.

I sit down at the table, careful not to upset her papers. "I know. But things are . . . Things are bad at their house. I think they all need a break."

"Bad, how?" Mom asks, sitting upright. "Jude, you know you can tell me anything."

"They fight a lot—Dallas's parents, I mean." It feels so good to finally tell an adult. Someone who might be able to *do* something about it. "Massive screaming matches. They swear a lot too."

"Oh dear."

"Yeah. And it's getting worse. I don't know what to do," I admit. "It's not like I can ask Dallas and his sisters to move in with us. I don't know if they would. Or if you'd even let them. But—"

"Jude."

I meet my mom's eyes.

"How long has this been going on?"

"A few years . . ." I look down again, pulling at a loose thread on my jeans. "But it keeps getting worse, and not better."

"Are they being abused?"

"Not that I know of," I answer honestly. "It's just been a lot of screaming at each other. Not so much Dallas and his sisters, as far as I know."

"Okay," she says, nodding. "They can come over for the whole weekend. I'll talk to their mom. Maybe we can figure something out. But, Jude." She sighs, reaching a hand across the table. I leave the thread alone to reach back. "You can't save everyone from everything. Sometimes, people just have to go through . . . whatever they're going through."

"I don't think their fights should be one of those things," I mutter.

"No, it shouldn't be. I agree. But I can't control what happens in someone else's house."

I nod, but I don't get it. Shouldn't we be doing everything in our power to help the people we love?

I send Dallas and Stevie a group text about the sleepover. Stevie leaves Dallas and I on read for the rest of the night, but we keep talking as if everything's normal.

• • •

Despite being MIA for a while, Stevie gets permission to join our sleepover. It's been long enough since we've spent time together outside of school. She's missed *two* Taco Tuesdays now.

Dallas says Aspen, Jersey, and Paris are grateful for a breather from their house too. The three of them spend the night in the guest room talking with one another, and I'm not surprised they don't want to join us. They're acting as if it's a sister getaway, even though Brooklyn ditched the house for some of her college friends and Holland is half a world away in Australia.

I hope their parents can figure it out. None of your kids wanting to spend time with you should be a wake-up call, letting you know something's really wrong.

Dallas, Stevie, and I decide to sleep in the living room. That way, no one gets left alone on the floor. We've made ourselves a fort too. It was fun building something together. Mom said it has to come down before everyone leaves tomorrow, but I don't mind. She even pulled out the Christmas twinkle lights for us to use.

We lie on our backs, staring up at the sheet ceiling.

"Where have you been?" I muster the courage to ask Stevie. I was planning on surprising her with the idea of the RSS, but she's been a little distant—and it feels like it's been *forever*.

Stevie plays with the edge of the blanket before she finally admits what's been going on. "Tessa wants me back. I don't know what to do."

"Tell her to screw off," I say immediately.

"Jude!"

I shoot Dallas a look and shrug. I'm not going to apologize. "Stevie, Tessa treated you like crap. She can't even handle someone *disagreeing* with her. Is that really who you want to be friends with?"

"It's more than that," Stevie tries to explain. "I know I've only talked badly about her, but she's also been a good friend to me."

"How?" I ask, scoffing.

"You don't know her like I do." Stevie frowns at the sheet ceiling. "She's not *all* bad. She's been a great friend, and she apologized. Do you know how hard it must have been for her to apologize?"

"I don't," I admit. "Because I don't think a friend who struggles to apologize is a friend I'd want."

"Me neither," Dallas whispers. "This sucks, Stevie. What are you going to do?"

"I—I don't know. Tessa doesn't want me hanging out with you two anymore, but . . ." Stevie sighs. "I was hoping we could save this conversation until tomorrow."

"Wow," I say.

Dallas lets out a low whistle. "Damn, Stevie."

"Are you breaking up with us?" I demand.

"Sort of? It's just . . . it's . . . Tessa makes me . . . feel important. And sometimes, I sort of feel left out with you both. You have so much history with each other that I don't get. And I don't . . . know. I miss Tessa." Stevie takes a deep breath. "I'm sorry."

I stare at the roof of our fort and let my mind swirl around. "Is this why you haven't been around much?"

"Yeah."

"So, you've been lying to us," I snap.

"No! No, I just . . ."

"Did you *really* have family stuff?"

"Yes, well, no, but—"

"Were you hoping that we'd just"—I wave a hand around in the air above me—"let it go?"

"No, I just—I don't—" Stevie starts and stalls beside me. She rubs her face, and I can't bring myself to look at her. "It's not like . . . it's . . . it's just . . . It's complicated, okay?"

"I don't think it sounds complicated," I mutter, crossing my arms over my chest. "You're choosing Tessa over us."

"It's not like that!" Stevie protests, but it's *exactly* like that. "You don't understand."

"I think we understand perfectly clear," I say, sitting up. "If you don't want to be friends with us anymore, then I think you should leave."

No one says anything for a moment, and then Stevie pulls out her phone. She fidgets with it, and I think I see her hands shake before she raises it to her ear. "Mom? Can you come pick me up?"

"So, it's official," I murmur. Dallas and I share a look, and then I crawl out of the fort. Dallas follows me.

"What just happened?" he hisses.

"I don't know," I admit. "But I think we just lost Stevie as a friend."

Dallas hugs himself, hovering at the edge of the kitchen. We share another look; this time, it's filled with lots of regret, confusion, and sadness. Without a word spoken between us, I know Dallas hates this as much as I do.

Stevie crawls out from the fort a few minutes later. "My mom will be here in twenty minutes."

"Okay," I barely manage.

She doesn't say anything else; she simply starts to pack up her stuff. She shoves her regular clothes into her backpack without folding them like she always does. Dallas and I can't do anything but watch, helpless and confused.

"This is so weird," Dallas whispers to me. I nod but don't respond. I don't know what else there is to say.

Stevie, Dallas, and I sit in the living room in silence for almost twenty minutes before there's a knock at the door. Stevie's almost finished putting on her shoes when my mother walks into the room.

"Jude, it's a little late for more friends."

"Um." I look at her and nod toward Stevie. "Stevie's going home, actually."

"Oh no!" Mom walks over. "Are you feeling okay, dear? Let me talk to your mother. Perhaps we can take care of you here or—"

"No, it's okay, Miss Winters," Stevie says quickly. At least she's still polite to my mother. "I'm just feeling homesick. Thank you so much for having me over, though."

Ha, I want to say. It's all fake. All of it. Stevie means none of it. She came here to break hearts.

Mom and Stevie chat for a moment, and then my mom talks to Stevie's mother. The entire time, Dallas and I continue to share looks between us. *This is uncomfortable. This is awkward. This is too much.*

"Come say goodbye, Jude," Mom calls out from the front porch.

"I'm okay."

"Jude, don't be rude," my mom hisses.

I swallow and then jog up to the front door to wave goodbye. Stevie doesn't look at us, but her mother waves back.

Mom closes the door and asks, "Do I want to know what that was really about?"

"No," I mumble. "It's fine."

It doesn't feel fine, though.

"Okay, well, don't stay up too late, okay?" Mom says, before leaving us alone to deal with the fallout.

Dallas and I curl up under the fort again, this time curling into each other. He grabs my hand. We don't talk for a while. It's hard, suddenly losing Stevie.

"I can't believe she did that," I whisper.

"Me neither," Dallas whispers back.

"I didn't even get a chance to tell her about the Rosedeen Safe Space," I add. My heart feels heavy, like someone's standing on it. "I thought she'd love that idea. I named it safe space because . . ."

"Yeah," Dallas whispers.

I wipe tears from the edges of my eyes and square my shoulders. "I'm going to the library after school on Monday."

Dallas squeezes my hand again. "I'll be there in spirit—you know I have to take care of Aspen. If Mom gets home early, I'll walk over. What about your grandparents' dinner?"

I scoff. "I think they can handle me missing *one* more dinner."

•   •   •

Turns out, they can't. Mom makes me go to dinner instead. But I tell her about my idea for the RSS on the car ride over, and it seems like she's impressed.

After I finish helping set the table, I find myself in the living room with Pops. He's watching the six o'clock news. One of the anchors is talking about a shelter that's overrun with animals and needs help.

"Maybe you should adopt a dog or a cat," I suggest to Pops. "I've always wanted a cat."

He grunts in response but doesn't look at me.

I sit awkwardly on the edge of a chair in the corner and feel like I'm shrinking. *Doesn't he want to get to know me?* And then another thought occurs to me: *Am I even letting him get to know me if I'm not sharing who I am with him?*

"**Jude**," Nan calls from the kitchen. "Come help put food on the table."

"Coming!" I reply. I look back at Pops. "Do you want to come help too?" I ask.

"I'm sure your grandmother has it under control," he says, without tearing his eyes from the TV.

Okay, then.

The rest of the evening goes exactly like it always does, and I'm quiet the entire ride home. I don't know what to say, but I know that if I have to go through another dinner like that again, I'm going to scream.

I can't hide anymore.

I don't *want* to hide anymore.

I just want to be me.

Why is that so much to ask?

CHAPTER 17

I give Mei a whole tray of Mom's brownies on Friday morning and ask if she'll drop me off at the public library after school. I unfold the note I asked Mom to write. Mei eyes it, then the brownies, and gives me a wink. "Sure thing, Jude. Anything for my favorite student."

"I knew it!" I tease, and she lets out a full-belly laugh.

I can't help but think of my grandparents—and the way they never laugh like that. Nan and Pops don't have any clue how angry I am at them. I'm exhausted; I don't want to pretend that nothing's wrong anymore.

It's like they think we solved our issues . . . by not talking about anything? *Yeah, right, Nan. Try again.* It's not my fault she just pretends I never brought up how she keeps making excuses for Pops. They teach us in school that talking helps, talking resolves things, talking is better than your fists, talking is better than using insults. Blah, blah, blah.

But then, Mom doesn't want me to talk about being queer. My grandmother doesn't want to talk about my grandfather being a jerk. And maybe if Dallas's parents would talk to each other nicely, they could sort something out. If talking really solves all problems, why aren't the adults doing it?

When I sit down beside Dallas, he holds up his old iPod. He's listening to Adele this morning, and I have no idea why. It's not like he's ever had his heart broken before.

"Hey," I mouth.

He gives me a nod and waits for his song to finish. "Hey."

• • •

At school, Stevie's wearing her hair pin straight again and a baby-pink skirt. It's been almost a week since our disaster of a sleepover, and it's still familiar and unfamiliar all at once. She's back to texting nonstop during English class, but I can't bring myself to be annoyed about it. I've been trying my best to avoid her, so of course, she walks past us without making eye contact.

Dallas and I share a sullen smile as I shut my locker.

"That was . . . yeah." I can't even bring myself to say words.

"I know what you mean," he says. I'm glad because I'm not even sure *I* know what I mean.

We settle into our usual table in the cafeteria and start talking about the latest Robin Hood update. It's an expanded retelling of *The Merry Adventures of Robin Hood* by Howard Pyle. My attention wavers when Dallas starts in on his usual rave about his favorite character.

". . . And you just *know* he's gonna do it."

"Stevie! Stand up straight, and get over here!"

The sound of Tessa's voice piques my interest, and I nudge Dallas to pay attention.

Stevie visibly straightens, squaring her shoulders, and walks briskly past our table toward Tessa. "Sorry, I—"

"No excuses, just hurry up," Tessa barks. She turns on her heel and walks toward her usual table. Stevie doesn't hesitate to follow.

"She looks miserable," Dallas comments quietly.

"Yeah, well, maybe she deserves it."

"Jude, you can't be serious," he says, giving me a disapproving look. "No one deserves to be treated like . . ."

"A lapdog?"

". . . *That.*"

"Do I have to remind you that she *ditched* us and *chose* Tessa?" I whisper.

Dallas sighs, as if he's accepting defeat. "Let's talk about something else."

By the end of the day, Dallas has forgiven me for being harsh at lunch. I settle in beside him on the bus, and he nods out the window. I lean forward and spot Stevie.

"Ugh," I mutter.

She looks kind of uncomfortable. I drop back into my seat.

So much for being my friend. Our friend.

"I miss her," Dallas whispers to me.

"We're better off without her," I declare. But I don't know if I even believe myself. Stevie gave us something special. Her laugh was contagious; when she listened to you, her eyes were so deep; and she always had a funny story to tell.

Dallas doesn't acknowledge what I said, but it's for the best. I explain I'm going to the library tonight, and he nods. "You've told me."

Somehow, now it's like Dallas and I don't know how to be around each other without Stevie.

I hate it.

She should've never joined us if she was going to ditch us just like that.

"Good luck," Dallas says when we turn onto the library's street.

"Thanks," I reply before standing up.

Fiddling with the strap on my backpack gives me a little comfort. I've never done anything like this, and my determination evaporates as we get closer. But it's not about me anymore. It's about everyone else. All the people who don't have a Dallas. Who need someone out there to understand them. I head to the front of the bus and thank Mei for the special stop.

"Any time, kid." Mei seems to hesitate, so I pause on the last step and look back. "You seem a little down, Jude. Everything okay?"

"Yeah," I say, but my smile is tight. I wonder if I look like my mother. Tight smiles are her specialty. "Mei, what did you think when I asked you to start calling me Jude?"

She glances in the mirrors before answering. "That it suits you much better."

"Really?"

"Really." At this moment, Mei's smile makes me feel invincible. "Whatever you want to do, Jude, remember that you're the bravest kid I know. Stay true to you, and don't let anyone try to knock you down."

"Thanks, Mei." I step off the bus, but I look back once more. She gives me another big smile and a thumbs-up.

• • •

When Dallas and I were around six, we used to come to the public library a lot. They had story time for kids every Saturday afternoon with Mr. Reyes, and Dallas and I *loved* it. The best days were when they let us act out scenes. I always wanted to be a dragon, even if there weren't any dragons in the story.

The library is exactly what a library should be: an old building in need of renovations, dusty wooden bookshelves, the smell of books, and reading pockets hidden among all the stories.

It's shared between Aberdeen Falls and Rose Creek now. Rose Creek has a small library of its own, but it doesn't have much. People usually have to wait to receive the more popular books from the Aberdeen Falls Library.

I don't wander through the shelves today, even though it's my favorite thing to do. Instead, I walk straight to the librarian's desk and wait for Miss Boyd to notice me. She graduated from college a few years ago and took over when Mr. Reyes retired. I don't know her that well since Mr. Reyes was still around when Dallas and I used to come in every Saturday, but she seems kind enough.

"Hi, dear, how can I help you today?"

My mouth goes dry. My mind is blank. I stare at her. She wears her black hair naturally, her glasses are a bright red, which is a contrast to her dark skin, and her dress looks soft. She seems like someone I can trust, but . . .

But there's something I didn't consider before I came here: I have to come out to Miss Boyd.

I haven't done that with a stranger before.

"I—"

"It's okay," she tells me, shuffling some papers together. "I won't judge you, and I keep secrets well."

I lean forward and keep my voice low. "I want to talk about gay things."

My cheeks immediately heat up. I can't believe I just said *that*. I slap a hand over my mouth. Miss Boyd doesn't laugh at me, though. Instead, she stops moving around her papers and gives me a solemn nod.

"Okay. Do you want fictional books? Educational books? Resources?"

"Um." I rub my hand over my face before glancing around. No one nearby has spared us another look. I take a deep breath. "Actually, I wanted to talk about a club or a safe space or . . . something."

Miss Boyd's face falls. "I'm sorry, we don't have anything like that here."

"But what if we did?"

"I would love that! What are you thinking of?" Miss Boyd asks me.

"What about a club for marginalized people?" I ask, wringing my hands.

"That's a great idea. Would you want to help run it?"

Just like that, all the worries leave me, and a smile breaks out over my face. "I can definitely help run it!"

"Perfect. I have some deadlines to deal with today, but maybe we can meet sometime next week and talk about our goals and what each of us can do to get something up and running?"

"Okay!"

"I'm Aly Boyd. Call me Aly."

"Jude."

"Nice to meet you, Jude."

And sometimes, it's just that easy.

Aly and I talk for a few minutes to organize a time to get together. Then I quietly say, "I've been calling this idea the Rosedeen Safe Space. Or the RSS for short."

"I like the name."

"I'll see you next week? And is it okay if I bring my friend with me?"

"I encourage it," Aly says, beaming. "I'll see you next week, Jude. Oh! Before I forget—what are your pronouns?"

My heart stops, filling up with so much love and affirmation. "They/them."

"They/them; got it. Mine are she/her." Aly gives me a nod and then turns to deal with an older person.

I head home with an extra skip in my step.

CHAPTER 18

"On another note, your English teacher called me earlier," Mom says once I get home and she's finished telling me my chores for the weekend.

"What? Why?"

"Mrs. Bayley is worried about you. She said you've been distracted in class and spending a lot of time on things unrelated to your schoolwork. She said there's a project you were supposed to be working on the past few weeks?"

I swallow. *Tattletale.* Shrugging, I say, "The RSS is important. And besides, I don't really get the project anyway."

"Jude." My mom heaves another sigh.

"What?"

"You can't just work on other things when you're supposed to be working on a project. And if it's too hard, you need to ask for help." She looks me in the eyes. "It's okay to get help. *Especially* since you have ADHD. You said at the start of last year that you could handle it, but if that's changed, we need to get you the support you need."

"I just . . . I can't concentrate in the classroom." I press my lips together before adding, "And I've been working on my project at home."

"And the talking in class without raising your hand?"

"I—" But there's no excuse for it. I simply never think to raise my hand. I blurt whatever comes to mind. Dallas has teased me about having no control of my own mouth.

Mom keeps going. "She also said you've had trouble staying quiet during individual work periods." At the mention of each new thing I've done wrong, I feel it in my stomach— like she's swinging a baseball bat right at my gut. I feel so called out.

I swallow, unsure what else to say. Mrs. Bayley isn't wrong—I do all those things.

"She recommended you start seeing Mr. Middleton again. His office is quiet, with minimal distractions, and he'll give you extra support on your work."

"I don't want to," I argue, but I know it's pointless. "It's just so *boring*."

"Jude . . ."

"It is! I can handle it, Mom. I don't need extra support," I protest.

"It's not up for discussion." Mom looks at me pointedly.

"That's not fair. We always discuss things first!"

"And you know I support your idea for this club, but if

that's what you're fixated on . . ." Mom sighs. "We might have to nix the idea."

"*Mom!*" I whine. I am so not above whining.

"We'll see how Mr. Middleton's help goes first," she decides. "Promise me you'll try harder to focus on your schoolwork?"

"Promise," I mumble.

This is *so* not the direction I expected this conversation to go.

Jogging up the stairs, I wonder when my ADHD will get better—and if it will ever feel manageable. I remember when I was first diagnosed; everything started to click into place, almost like when I first heard the definition of *nonbinary*. It was a rush of *Oh, this is so me.*

I worked with Mr. Middleton for most of fifth grade, then when sixth grade started, I asked if I could handle it on my own. But the work *is* getting harder, and I can feel my attention wandering more and more these days.

I decide to give Dallas a call to see if he wants to come over. He's been busier lately, hanging out with his sisters and babysitting Aspen more nights a week. This week, he's been listening to Taylor Swift's *folklore* and *evermore* albums, which means he's a little depressed and needs a pick-me-up.

I don't know if there's something other than his parents,

because as far as I can tell, the fighting has stopped. Maybe they're working things out. Either way, I'm missing Dallas more than usual.

I tap my foot repeatedly on the floor while I wait for him to pick up, because I can't imagine a life without Dallas. He's my *person*. And if he's pulling away from me like Stevie did . . .

"Hey," Dallas says finally. "Right now isn't the best time."

I deflate. "Oh, okay. Is everything all right?"

"No. Mom and Dad announced their divorce."

"Oh, sugar." Except I don't say *sugar*. The word slips out of my mouth before I can stop it. Mom says that whenever she's surprised. And for once, Dallas doesn't scold me. I rub the back of my neck and ask, "Are you okay?"

"Mostly, yeah." Dallas sighs. "It's not like I didn't see this coming. It's just . . . weird that it finally happened, y'know?"

"Oh, Dal." I close my eyes, settling onto my bed. "It's okay to be upset. Everything is going to change, and you have every right to feel however you do."

"I didn't even think of the changes," Dallas admits. "Two houses, two holidays, two . . . everything."

"Yeah. But that's not the worst thing in the world. Double the gifts for your birthday," I point out. "And no more screaming and fighting."

"Yeah," Dallas breathes into the phone. "No more

screaming and fighting. I guess I can't believe that's over. I don't know. I feel messed up, Jude. So, so messed up."

"What do you need?" I ask, fidgeting with the end of the blanket on my bed.

"A distraction, please." Dallas makes a strange noise, and I realize he's crying. The only time I've ever seen Dallas cry was when his grandmother passed away. "How did it go at the library?"

"Oh! Pretty well, actually," I say, hoping he'll want to talk more about the club.

I know it's all I've been thinking about lately—even thoughts of Stevie seem scarce. I still miss her, though, more than I want to admit.

I talk about the library for a few minutes, hoping something will excite Dallas. Instead, his voice is quiet and flat when he says, "That's great, Jude."

Now I feel like I'm annoying him. "Why don't you tell me a secret?"

He laughs. "As if I have any from you." But there's a hesitation in his voice. He adds, "Actually, I do have one."

"How could you possibly have a secret from me?" I joke, but I'm nervous. Is he going to tell me something bad? Like maybe I'm not enough for him anymore?

"I texted Stevie yesterday. She hasn't replied."

"Did you really expect her to?" I ask, shifting on my bed so I have a pillow under my head. I don't get why Dallas texted Stevie; she made her choice, and it wasn't us.

Dallas sniffs again and then blows his nose. I would usually tease him that it's gross how loud he is, but I let it slide this time.

"No, I guess not," he says. "I just don't get it."

"Me neither. Tessa is awful, and I don't really understand why Stevie would want to hang around someone like that." After a minute of silence, I say, "Hey, Dallas?"

"Hmm?"

"Do you think we were just temporary friends for her? Like she never really wanted to be our friend, but it was just convenient?"

"I guess we were. But it really felt like she was . . ."

"One of us?"

"Yeah. Yeah, it really did. I'll let you know if she texts me back."

"Don't hold your breath."

"Jude," he says in that tone that means I'm in trouble. "You can't be so callous about Stevie leaving . . . You must be hurt too."

"I—I am," I admit, swallowing hard. I stare at my ceiling, looking at all the glow-in-the-dark star stickers Dallas helped me put up two years ago. I trace the biggest star with my eyes. "It's just . . . She left us. And for what? Tessa? You can't seriously tell me that makes any sense to you."

"It doesn't," Dallas admits. "We're way better at being friends than Tessa is. We aren't mean *T. rex*es that are willing to eat anyone in their way."

I laugh at the idea of Tessa as a *T. rex* with little arms. Dallas sounds almost back to normal when we start an elaborate story about Tessa the *T. rex* eating and destroying everything in her path.

So, maybe Stevie used us for a little while, but at least Dallas and I will be okay just us again.

"And then," I say dramatically, "she gets her nose stuck in the crack of the building and can't push herself out because her arms are so little!"

Dallas and I both giggle.

"You know, Stevie is missing out on the greatest thing that could've happened to her!" Dallas says. "I know you're the greatest thing that happened to me. Being your best friend makes me feel like I can tackle a *T. rex* any day."

"Ohmigod, Dal-laaaas!" I squeal, grinning. "That was so cute! Thank you."

"It's true. I should go soon. But thanks for calling. It always helps."

"Well, I'm only a text away if you need me." I rub

my nose. "And I'm sorry about your parents. It sucks."

"It *does* suck."

We talk for a little longer before we hang up, and I'm left looking at my phone screen. I scroll through old messages from Stevie. *Could I have seen this coming?* I don't know. I really don't. Everything seemed normal and fine until a couple of weeks before she ditched us.

I'm probably making a colossal error.

Probably.

But I'm making it anyway.

I miss you, I type.

Then I delete the text without sending it. How could I be so careless? If she wasn't going to reply to Dallas, she definitely isn't going to reply to me.

• • •

In the morning, I notice that it was almost midnight when I received a missed call from Stevie. It's like she read my mind.

But I don't call back.

CHAPTER 19

After school on Wednesday, I go back to the public library. Dallas has to go home first, so he's going to join us for the second half of the meeting.

"Hi," I say, more shyly than I expect.

Aly looks up from her desk and gives me a wide smile. "Jude! I'm so excited you're here. I've been looking forward to this all week. I booked us the meeting room, so if you want to head in now, I'll just be a few minutes."

"Okay!" I say, feeling more confident. "I'm excited too."

I let myself into the meeting room, happily surprised to find some muffins and a little coffee and tea station. I set my backpack down and pull out my folder of notes and ideas.

As I'm making myself some tea, I hear Aly talking to someone outside the door.

"Yeah, that sounds great. I'll let them know you'd like to join the meeting." Aly pokes her head in. "Think we have room for one more?"

I'm too overwhelmed by her perfect use of my pronouns to do anything but nod.

"Sweet." She leans back out and says, "They say it's okay. Come on in."

I stir sugar into my tea and give our newcomer a warm smile.

"Hi," I say to the older white man, who's probably close to sixty.

His smile is missing at least two teeth. Maybe he's older than I thought.

Aly comes in and shuts the door behind her. "I was telling Barnaby about your idea, and he just loves it. He wants to help out. He's been volunteering at the library most weekdays since he retired a few years ago."

"I didn't have anything like this when I was your age," Barnaby says, his voice gruffer than I expect. He takes a seat. "I didn't have any gay friends then either, because it wasn't safe for many of us to come out, and I was picked on a lot for being queer. But I think what you want to do with this club is great, and I'd be honored to help with it."

I laugh. He's delightful. "That's really cool of you."

Aly settles into her seat. "All right, Jude, what do you think we should focus on first?"

"A mission statement," I say, feeling professional. "Then I'd like to write up some rules and an agreement for members to sign. Something about promising to keep the stuff we talk about confidential." I pull a piece of paper from my binder. "I drafted something earlier today."

"I like them," Barnaby says to Aly, and his grin stretches the wrinkles on his cheeks. "Jude, right? You are a natural businessperson."

He doesn't miss a beat, doesn't mess up with gendered words. And the tears hit me instantly. I don't mean to cry. I don't want them to think I'm a crybaby, and I *really* want to remain professional. But the tears burn, and I can't stop them.

"Did I do something wrong?" Barnaby asks Aly.

"Sweetheart, what's going on?" Aly says to me.

"He didn't— He didn't misgender me— And— and my grandparents don't— They can't see— They can't get it." It all comes out between broken sobs.

During the first meeting of the Rosedeen Safe Space, I cry harder than I have in a long, long time. It takes me almost five minutes before I start to calm down.

"Let it out. It's okay. It's going to be okay," Aly says softly.

"I'm so sorry about your grandparents, Jude," Barnaby says. "That must be hard."

Between sniffs, I finally manage to string some words together. "Sorry, that was super unprofessional of me."

Aly and Barnaby share a look. Aly shakes her head, passing me another tissue. "Don't worry. Isn't that the very point of creating a safe space? So people don't have to hide anymore?"

I sniff and nod. "Yeah. Yeah, I guess you're right. It's hard. My mom knows, but she doesn't want me to come out to my grandparents. She thinks it'll be too complicated and hard for them to understand that I'm not a girl or a boy."

"I understand," Barnaby says, nodding. "Back in my day, nonbinary folks weren't talked about much. That doesn't mean there weren't nonbinary folks, just that it wasn't talked about."

"Yeah," I manage to say, lip trembling. That's what my mom keeps telling me when she reminds me why I shouldn't come out to my grandparents. She says, *It isn't something they have experience with.*

"That's not to say your grandparents couldn't possibly understand," Barnaby continues. "It might take them longer to get it, but . . . anyone worth their salt will accept and love you for who you are."

"Th-thank you," I whisper. "I guess it's hard to know what they'll think unless I tell them."

"Your mother is probably trying her best to protect you," Aly points out. She holds her hand out for me. I take it and close my eyes. "She can't possibly know how hard this is for you, not unless you tell her."

I nod. "Yeah. I've tried. She just . . . doesn't seem to *get it.*"

"Sorry," Aly and Barnaby say in unison.

I nod. "Thanks. Um, should we continue with the meeting?"

"Absolutely!" Aly says, clapping her hands. "So, mission statement?"

I take a deep breath and pick my paper up again. "I have a rough draft here."

I don't tell them I wrote it in Mrs. Bayley's class instead of doing my homework.

They both read it over, and we spend the next half hour reworking it to come up with something more substantial and succinct than my original one.

"Want to read us the final version?" Aly asks, pushing the piece of paper toward me.

"'The official mission statement of the newly created Rosedeen Safe Space is as follows,'" I start. "'To promote acceptance and provide a safe support group for marginalized people who share a common vision of social equality and equity.'"

Barnaby smiles. "I'm learning so much already."

"Me too," I whisper, looking down at our mission statement. I feel an overwhelming sense of pride rush through me. At least, I think this is what pride feels like. It's as if the mission statement was written on my heart, and now that we've got it down on paper, I could just hug it tight.

"What's next?" Barnaby asks.

"Rules," I say. I already feel right about this. "Like, this is a judgment-free zone, and everything that's shared here stays here. Anonymously."

"That's a great start," Aly says, scribbling it down. "What else?"

"People do not have to share anything with the group, but they are encouraged to," Barnaby suggests.

We're on the fifth and final rule when there's a knock at the door and Dallas sticks his head into the room. "Hi. I'm Dallas—a friend of Jude's. May I join?"

"Of course!" Aly says.

He sits beside me, and I quickly introduce everyone.

"Sorry about not making it earlier," Dallas says. "I had to babysit my little sister."

"We're just about finished here," Aly says, smiling. "But we would love your help with making posters. Jude says you're really handy when it comes to the computer. We have a mock-up done on Canva; would you be able to look at it?"

"Sure," Dallas says.

Barnaby speaks up. "I'd like to include a quote by Micah Bazant in honor of Marsha P. Johnson on it: 'No pride for some of us without liberation for all of us.' I don't know if you kids know about her, but Marsha Johnson was a huge part of queer history. Back in, oh, 1969, I think it was. She helped start the Stonewall Riots in New York City."

"Stonewall?" Dallas asks, looking at me curiously. I shrug because this is news to me as well.

Barnaby smiles, his wrinkles folding in on themselves, but his smile doesn't meet his eyes. "Stonewall is an inn and bar in New York that was popular with queer folks in the late sixties. It was the only bar in New York where gay people were allowed to dance with one another. The police raided it—meaning they came in and started arresting people on questionable charges. Marsha, like others in the gay community, was tired of being targeted. So, a bunch of them started to riot, basically, and fought against the police. It lasted for days, and people consider it a huge turning point for gay people everywhere."

"Kind of like the Black Lives Matter protests, but for queer people?" I ask.

"Exactly. Marsha P. Johnson is a name you should remember. She made change happen."

"We also had our own things like that in Canada. Some police raided a place in Montreal in the early nineties. It's often referred to as Montreal's Stonewall," Aly says. "And similar raids happened in Toronto too. It's interesting how history keeps repeating itself, but at least we're moving forward."

"Sometimes it feels like we're going backward at the same time. What about the whole Toronto Public Library thing?" I ask. "I remember reading that they were letting a transphobic person speak and use their space. When I learned what that meant, Mom had to calm me down. I wasn't even aware I was nonbinary then. I just knew it was hateful."

Aly ducks her head and nods. "Yeah. That was rough. I protested it with two friends of mine. I was still in school to be a librarian at the time."

"Oh, wow," I murmur. Barnaby looks impressed with Aly.

Dallas wrinkles his nose. "How do you feel about it now, as a librarian?"

"It was a difficult time, and I don't agree with how they handled that situation at all. They should never have let that awful woman use their facilities. Yes, the library is a safe place for everyone, but it shouldn't allow people who are going to spout hate and discrimination against a marginalized community."

"Thanks," I say, smiling a little. "I did think about that earlier—whether having this club at the library was the best idea."

"I want this to be a place where people can be themselves," says Aly.

"Me too."

And soon enough, the first official meeting of the RSS is over.

. . .

By the next Wednesday, the RSS is starting to feel even more real.

"These posters look amazing!" I gush as we walk down the hall toward the school exit.

"Aly said that too," Dallas says, and I swear he's blushing. "I think they turned out surprisingly good. She printed a bunch of color copies off for me, and I was hoping you'd want to help me put them up today?"

"Definitely!"

"She and Barnaby are going to put them up in Rose Creek, so we just have to worry about Aberdeen."

"Perfect," I say. And for a moment, everything feels like it's settling into place.

We spend a couple of hours after school walking around downtown, postering. We're putting up the last poster in the window of the local diner when Dallas says, "Is that Stevie and Tessa?"

I follow his gaze and freeze. They're coming out of the movie theater. I grab Dallas's wrist to pull him out of sight, but Stevie sees us anyway.

She tosses her head back and laughs loudly. It really stings. How can she prefer the company of Tessa over us? Weren't we good enough for her?

Dallas leads me away from the diner's front door and asks, "Are you okay?"

"Yeah. Yeah, I— Yeah." I can't tear my eyes off them.

Something's there, screaming to get out, and when I meet Dallas's eyes, I know he understands.

"You okay?" he asks again, this time a little quieter.

I'm trying not to feel completely devastated right now. "I don't know."

But it's another reminder how short our friendship was, and how she didn't choose us. I think back to that missed call and can't help but wonder: What if Tessa put her up to prank calling me as revenge? *How did I not think of that before?*

"Come on. Let's head home," Dallas says.

I nod, but when I look back at Stevie and Tessa, my heart sinks, and the monster inside me rears up. A whirlpool of emotions I can't name are spinning so quickly I can't catch them and pin them down.

"Dallas, I—I don't get why she didn't stay."

"I know," he murmurs. He grabs my hand and takes me around the corner. He doesn't say much else, and we walk home in broken silence.

CHAPTER 20

Stevie laughing with Tessa churns around in my head. The disappointment that fills me is unbearable. I want to crawl out of my own skin; I want to be someone else, live a different life. It doesn't make sense. At first, she looked so miserable being friends with Tessa again, and now—now she's *laughing*? Is she trying to twist the dagger in my heart?

I just wish she had wanted to be my friend *more*. Seeing her with Tessa—laughing as if nothing's wrong—feels awful. It's not fair.

Why did she leave me?

Stevie is wicked cool. I admired her when she was her toughest, respected her when she was at her weakest, and adored her when we were friends. Somehow through it all, she managed to snag a piece of my heart, even if she doesn't know exactly who she wants to be yet.

I love that she snorts when she laughs really hard, and the way she tucks and untucks her hair behind her ear. It used to bother me, but now it's just another piece of who she is. I like how her eyes light up when she gets to the good part of a story. And I love that she never expected me to be anyone but myself.

I remember when we had our last sleepover before everything became ruined like a book in the rain. Dallas fell asleep first, and Stevie asked me if I think karma exists.

"I think so," I told her. "I think there are some energies in the universe that try to balance everything out."

"I wonder how I'm doing," Stevie whispered.

Great, I wanted to tell her. *You've changed my life for the better.*

But I stayed silent. I don't know why; maybe I wasn't ready to share all my cards yet. Maybe I knew it was only temporary.

• • •

Admitting how much I loved being Stevie's friend is hard enough, but having to keep seeing her with Tessa is worse. They're attached at the hip, and the only time I've seen them apart since that day downtown is when we're assigned separate groups in health class. Tessa, unfortunately, is in my group.

"Okay," she says, taking charge without being asked. "I vote we do our project on positive body image, and—"

I tune her out, doodling in my notebook. I draw a little bunny holding a heart. It's not exactly the best doodle, but I draw some carrots around him, and it's kind of cute.

"Do you have that, *Jude*?"

I look up at the sound of my deadname. *Jude,* I correct immediately in my head. I rewrite her question, but I can't capture the snotty tone. Bristling, I inhale to keep my cool. "It's Jude."

"Right, right, of course." She rolls her eyes. "Because everyone can just change their name willy-nilly."

My head jerks back with the shock of it. I glance at the other group members, but they're looking away—avoiding any confrontation with Tessa.

"Mrs. Reynolds," I call out.

"Where's your hand, Jude?" Mrs. Reynolds asks, sounding tired.

"Sorry." I stick my hand in the air.

"Yes?" she asks.

"I would like a new group," I tell her boldly. "I can't work with Tessa."

"No group changes," Mrs. Reynolds says, shaking her head.

"She refuses to call me Jude."

"Call **them** Jude," Mrs. Reynolds says, except she uses the wrong pronoun.

And then she's gone.

I feel a pit growing in my stomach. No one can help me now.

"You're such a baby," Tessa says, scoffing. "Tattling? You won't be able to handle the real world with that soft skin, *Jude*."

This time she says the right name, but with such an attitude it still feels wrong. What else can I do? I already tried explaining things to Mrs. Reynolds. *I* know who I am, and that's all I can control. Right? That's what Mom tells me.

But I can't stay quiet.

"You're a brat, Tessa," I say. Except *brat* isn't the word I use. I can't believe the word that slips right out of my mouth. The other members of our group gasp, looking at Tessa to see her reaction.

She's calm when she says, "You'll regret that."

"Will I?" I say before I can stop myself. "Because I don't think I will. It's true, and we both know it. You can't even respect my name, which is the bare minimum of human decency."

Tessa laughs, but it's not funny. "I don't really care what you want to call yourself. You know what you'll always be? A loser."

"At least people like me for me. They're just afraid of you."

"You think Stevie liked you? She was forced to hang out with you and spent the entire time begging me to forgive her." Tessa's eyes latch on to me as I digest her words. "She *hated* that you prank called me."

My heart sinks. Stevie was begging for Tessa's forgiveness? Did she really hate hanging out with us that much?

Tessa sees the hurt on my face and thinks she won.

My eyes flicker toward Stevie, who has her head down, and I remember how she put the progress flag in my hands. How she painted my nails orange. How hard we laughed together.

I quietly say, "She's better than you in every way, and that's why you keep her close."

It's almost as if I hit her right where it hurts most, because Tessa looks visibly upset. She puts her hand up, and Mrs. Reynolds comes over. Tessa gives me a smirk before pouting to the teacher. "I can't work with Jude, Mrs. Reynolds. It's a clash of personalities. Can I be in Stevie's group instead?"

"All right," Mrs. Reynolds says, motioning for Tessa to join Stevie's group on the other side of the classroom.

I squawk in protest, but it doesn't matter. Tessa's won this round after all. She packs up her stuff and joins Stevie, who looks surprised. Our eyes meet, and I hope she knows she's better than this.

There's more to Stevie than just being Tessa's lapdog. I *know* it, even if no one else does.

CHAPTER 21

Dallas and I go to the movies on Sunday, Mom's treat. She told us to quit moping around and go do something. We decided on a double feature of two queer movies: *The Love Interest* and *Hazel Bly*. We're on the edge of our seats the entire time, and Dallas whispers his thoughts to me through both of them. I try to tell him to quit it, but I end up grabbing his hand for the last half of the second movie. It's more intense than I was expecting, and I cry at least twice.

When we get out of *Hazel Bly*, I'm feeling both excited and exhausted. Dallas chatters on about his favorite part until we reach the bathrooms.

"Be right back, Jude," Dallas says, walking into the bathroom.

I start to follow him toward the bathrooms, then hesitate.

Why should I have to choose a gender that doesn't fit me just to use the washroom?

"Hey, are you okay?"

I turn around to see Stevie standing there. She looks

nervous, and I can't blame her. "What do you want?" I ask, crossing my arms.

"Um, nothing. Sorry. I just—I saw you in the *Hazel Bly* theater with Dallas. Just . . ." Stevie looks down at her feet. "I'm here with my mom. I didn't have to use the bathroom, so . . ."

"So . . ." What else can we talk about? It's not like we're friends anymore.

"They have a family bathroom now too. It's a single stall," Stevie says, as if she can read my mind. I guess for a while there, she could. I look to where she's pointing.

"Th-thanks," I stammer. I run a hand through my hair and shake my head. "Stevie, what do you expect? That Dallas and I aren't hurt? That it wasn't a slap in the face that you went back to Terrible Tessa?"

Stevie's eyes widen, and her lower lip trembles. "Jude, you have to understand . . . I didn't have much choice."

"You *always* have a choice." I shake my head.

Dallas comes out of the bathroom, and I see him almost miss a step when he spots Stevie standing with me. He slides up beside me and says, "Stevie."

"Dallas." She echoes his curt tone. "I guess I'll be going . . ."

"Yeah, that's probably for the best." I turn to Dallas. "She was just telling me there's a single bathroom over there."

"What . . ." Dallas starts, but then Stevie's walking away, toward her mother. She doesn't look back. ". . . did I miss?"

"Nothing," I reply. "I'll be right back, okay?"

Then I leave Dallas standing there as I rush toward the family bathroom. Luckily, no one's in it. I slam the door shut and lock it behind me. Leaning against the bathroom door, I take a few deep breaths.

I've tried to be relaxed about the whole Stevie thing. Dallas and I went back to our usual routine, acting like we weren't missing a third of us. But seeing her and having her read me like that . . . It hurts.

"Sorry," I say to Dallas when I meet up with him again. He glares at me and doesn't say anything. "Sorry! I panicked. I didn't know what to do. It's not like we were talking."

"You weren't rude to her, were you?" Dallas demands. "Because if she wanted to be our friend again and—"

"And what?" I ask. "And she wanted to come crawling back, we'd accept her? No way, Dal. Come on. She abandoned us for Tessa. Aren't you a little bit angry?"

"Of course I'm angry!" Dallas says, raising his voice slightly. "But, Jude, I would rather have Stevie back as our friend than not have her at all. Don't you get that? Can't you get that?"

"I guess."

But I don't know. How can Dallas be okay with letting Stevie back in our lives? What if she ghosts us every time Tessa comes calling? Isn't he worried it could happen again? I look at him and feel completely drained.

"Can we go home now?"

"I'll call my sister for a ride," Dallas says. "I don't feel like walking."

"Me neither."

●　●　●

Dallas and I opt not to talk about Stevie anymore, and it seems to work for us. Instead, we throw all our energy into making the RSS happen.

Two days later, we're walking to the library when we spot Tessa and Stevie looking at one of the RSS posters. Then Tessa reaches up and yanks it down. Dallas and I share a shocked expression as they walk away, talking to each other as if they hadn't just ripped my heart and soul from the bulletin board.

"Wow" is all Dallas manages.

I say nothing at all.

He prints off some new posters to replace that one and a few others that get torn down here and there, and I spend some time studying different sexualities and genders. I don't want to be totally clueless in front of the other members. Another week without Stevie passes as Dallas works through

JoJo Levesque's new album. When he finishes the latest Song of the Day, he wraps the headphone cord around his iPod and tucks it away. I was worried because he usually listens to her classic song "Leave (Get Out)" when his parents' fighting is frustrating him, but yesterday he assured me he just hasn't had time to listen to her new stuff outside of the mornings.

"So, you're telling me there's a difference between bisexual and pansexual?" Dallas asks me as he peers at the article I'm reading on my phone. "I thought they basically mean the same thing."

"No, actually, they don't. Bi means two or more genders—genders are not specified but tend to have an impact on attraction. And pansexuality is when someone is into a person *regardless* of their gender." I scroll down my phone some more. "The difference might be minor to you and me, but it matters to people who choose these labels. I'm still bisexual, I think."

"Yeah?" Dallas asks, leaning over to read from my screen. "I'm still gay."

I laugh. "Duh."

"I didn't realize there were so many different sexualities," Dallas says.

"Me neither," I admit. "It's a good thing we're creating a safe space, though. We can learn all this stuff!"

Dallas laughs. "You know, if you put half the amount of effort into school as you do with this club, you'd be finished with all your assignments by now."

I cringe. "Not you too! Am I protected from anybody?"

"I'm just saying! I saw you drawing a logo for the club instead of writing down the math questions," Dallas says. And, wow, do I ever feel called out.

I stick my tongue out at him. "Whatever. It's only math. Besides, next week I'm starting back up with Mr. Middleton."

"You are?"

"Yeah. Mom and Mrs. Bayley agreed it's for the best a while ago. We were just waiting for Mr. Middleton to make room in his schedule for me. But yeah, turns out I can't control my ADHD." I shrug. "I like Mr. Middleton, though. He's funny."

"Good," Dallas says. He pauses before adding, "But I'll miss having class with you."

"You'll still have *some* classes with me. Just not all." I nudge him. "Anyway, tell me. How are things at home?"

"Nice subject change." Dallas grins at me. "Better, actually. It's quiet. It was a little weird at first, but it's going great now that my dad's moved out. He's crashing at a friend's house until he can find his own place. Can I admit something awful?"

"Always."

"And you won't judge me?"

"I won't judge you."

"Absolute?"

"Absolute," I confirm.

"I think I like it better without my dad around." Dallas lets out a deep breath and covers his face. "Does that make me the worst person you know?"

"Tessa still has that title," I point out, "for being herself. But no, I think it makes sense. Your dad was causing a lot of problems, especially for your mother."

"He really was."

"So it doesn't surprise me it's nicer without him around." I elbow Dallas gently. "Don't beat yourself up about it, okay?"

"Okay." Dallas gives me the smallest smile. "Thanks, Jude. I'm glad I have you."

And that deserves a big bear hug. I shove my phone into the pocket of my hoodie and pull him in close. He grumbles about it for a solid second and a half before hugging me tighter than he ever has before.

CHAPTER 22

Monday is a little unusual for me. I'm called out of science class to sit with Mr. Middleton and get extra help. He's an older guy who cracks a few jokes that genuinely make me laugh before he tells me to sit down at a desk. I notice his earlobes are attached right to his head.

"Jude, Jude, Jude," he says, grinning. His smile is lopsided but instantly makes me feel at ease. He comes around to lean against the front of his desk. "So, we meet again."

"So, we do." I grin at him. "I guess I'm not the ADHD master after all, huh?"

"No one really is," he says with a wink. "Why don't we start with your English project, yeah?"

It's easier to work when someone's watching your every move. I work harder at staying on task, even if my mind wanders about the upcoming RSS meeting.

A few times, Mr. Middleton has to pull my attention to the assignment, but overall, I find it easier to work with him than on my own in the busy classroom.

I wonder if Stevie will notice I'm missing. Will she care?

"Jude! Back here," Mr. Middleton calls, snapping me out of my thoughts again.

I laugh and put my head down.

Getting extra support for my ADHD means I don't have to do tests with the class anymore, so I'm happy. There aren't as many distractions in Mr. Middleton's office, and he doesn't do that annoying hovering thing. When I worked with him before, he would sometimes sit beside me to read out the questions, and occasionally he'd help me write down my answers. I found it easier to verbalize my responses than write them down. Mr. Middleton says that's an ADHD thing too.

I'm staring out the window when Mr. Middleton coughs. I glance over at him, and he raises an eyebrow. Right, work.

But it's a lost cause. My concentration is gone.

"Mr. Middleton?" I ask, hand slightly raised. I'm getting a bit better at that stuff. He nods in my direction. "Could I maybe . . . go for a walk?"

"A walk." Mr. Middleton eyes me. "Do you think it'll help you focus?"

"Yeah, maybe. I don't know. You said sometimes getting up and walking around helps."

He laughs. "That I did. All right, I'll give you a hall pass. You need to be back within five minutes, and you can't disrupt anyone else. Just quietly walk the halls, okay?"

"You're the best!" I say, swinging out of my chair. I grab the hall pass from him, smiling when I realize he's the first person to understand my need to stretch, to get out of one place and move into another.

Five minutes later, I'm about to circle back to Mr. Middleton's office when I see Stevie standing at her locker. I hesitate, debating whether it's a good idea or not before I walk over. I want to confront her about tearing down the RSS poster, but as I get closer to her, my courage starts to fade.

"Hi," I whisper.

"Hi!" Stevie says, surprised. She shifts on her feet. "Jude. Hi. I forgot my textbook, so I was just getting it."

"Cool." I rub my hands together. "Mr. Middleton let me go for a little walk to clear my head."

"That's nice." Stevie frowns. "Listen, I didn't mean to completely abandon you like that, but —"

"Stevie? I don't really want to hear your excuses," I tell her. "I just want to know . . . Was it all fake? A facade?"

"No. It really wasn't. I loved being friends with you."

"But . . ."

"But Tessa's Tessa."

"Right. Okay." I can feel the tears press at the corners of my eyes. I think of how Tessa tore down our poster. "Well, if you ever need a real friend, don't look in my direction. Apparently, I'm only worthy of friendship when it's temporary."

I step back and turn around quickly, heading for Mr. Middleton's office. I don't look behind me.

I shouldn't have said anything, shouldn't have shown her I still care. But I *do* still care, and I don't even know why.

Back in Mr. Middleton's room, I take my seat and throw myself into my assignment. I surprise myself when I finish before the bell. I hand it in to him and quietly say, "Thanks for letting me go for that walk."

"Hey, anything that will help you focus like you did just now." Mr. Middleton gives me a kind smile. "I'm here to support you, Jude. Not make life more complicated."

"Thanks." I pause before adding, "I'm glad I have you in my corner."

We fist-bump, and then I leave.

I want to find Dallas and tell him I spoke with Stevie, and I don't think we're getting our friend back anytime soon.

CHAPTER 23

"Do we *have* to go?" I whine to my mother, who just hands me my sweater. I yank it on even though I'm hoping she'll say no, that we can stay home and have some pizza. She gives me a pointed look, and I shove my boots on. "I'm exhausted today, plus I haven't complained about the last *three* dinners."

"Mm-hmm. What's the next excuse?"

"No, really! Mr. Middleton's a hard-butt!" Except I don't say *butt*.

My mother looks outright scandalized. *"Jude. Language."*

"Uh, sorry." I don't tell her Mr. Middleton called himself that and I'm just repeating his words. "But he makes me work through the *whole* class."

"That's what you're supposed to be doing," my mother points out.

"Ugh."

We don't talk once we get in the car. I stare out the window, watching everything fly by in a blur, until we pull into my grandparents' driveway.

I try one more time. "Can't you get me out of these dinners?"

"Unfortunately for you, your grandparents love you," my mom says, sarcasm dripping from her words. She puts her hand on my shoulder. "C'mon, kiddo. The sooner we're in there, the sooner we're out of there."

I snort. Usually, my mom acts like she doesn't mind these dinners, but every so often, she'll show me a peek into her thoughts, and I remember she dreads them as much as I do.

We walk into my grandparents' house and do the usual greetings. My grandmother rushes back into the kitchen when a timer goes off, and once again Pops doesn't even bother getting up from the living room chair to say hello.

"**Jude**, set the table, please," Nan says.

Except I don't hear *Jude*. I cringe, glancing at my mother. She doesn't seem to notice the difference. My stomach sinks further. How many more times will I have to hear my dead-name? To pretend she called me Jude?

I close my eyes, take a deep breath, and start to set the table. It's okay. Everything is okay.

"You know, ever since you set up the Netflix account for us, Pops has been addicted," Nan tells me. "He loves that TV now."

I think Nan wants me to feel good about this, but instead my jaw stiffens and I try to remember to smile. "That's great!"

"He's always going on about some new show," Nan continues. "You were right, **Jude**."

Will I ever hear this from Pops? Probably not. I glance into the living room, where he sits watching an old basketball game. He shouts something at the TV, then taps his cup against the side table. "Betty, I need a refill."

"Coming," Nan says.

I set a fork down and watch as she pours him another drink.

"You okay, kid?" Mom asks, placing some buns on the table.

"Yeah," I murmur, but I think we both know I'm not.

After dinner, Pops tells me to put a record on. I don't really have any idea what I'm looking for until I find an old Beatles album. I glance at my mom, who is deep in conversation with Nan, before I pull it out and set up the record player.

"Hey Jude" starts playing through the speakers. Mom immediately meets my eyes and gives me a warning look, but I ignore her and go into the living room with Pops.

"How's this?" I ask, sitting down on the blue chair.

"Can't go wrong with the Beatles," Pop says. "Especially 'Hey Jude.'"

And for a moment, things feel all right.

But I count seventeen times they use the wrong name, forty-six times they use the wrong pronouns, and ten times they use a gendered term to describe me. I text Dallas the stats, and he sends me back seventy-four heart emojis.

I could cry.

• • •

It's Wednesday afternoon when Mom comes home from grocery shopping. She carries in four bags on her own before I run to put shoes on and help with the rest. There's not much left, so it's an easy chore to put everything away.

I'm putting the taco kit in the cupboard when Mom says, "I ran into Stevie's mother at the grocery store."

I freeze, waiting for more. It's coming, I just know it.

"She said it was too bad you kids were in a fight," Mom continues. *There it is.* "Is that why Stevie left the sleepover and hasn't been joining us for Taco Tuesdays?"

"Um," I start, because it's so complicated. Then the whole story comes tumbling out before I can stop myself.

". . . And that's why we're not friends anymore."

Mom nods toward the living room. "Why don't we go sit down?"

"Okay." I follow her, settling in with my legs up on the chair. I'm trying my best not to cry, but it's hard. "I don't know what to do. I'm so angry, but . . ."

"But you miss Stevie," Mom concludes for me. I nod, and she gives my hand a little squeeze. "Friendships can be tough, but sometimes it's good to have speed bumps. Your friendship might be stronger in the end because of this."

"But—did you not hear me? We're not friends anymore."

"It sounds to me like Stevie was put in a difficult position by Tessa."

"But Tessa made it seem like Stevie was begging to come back," I grumble.

"Hmm, does that sound like the Stevie you know?"

I shake my head in response, because *no*, it doesn't sound like the Stevie I know. Stevie was so fragile when she got away from Tessa. She was stronger, braver, and much more relaxed around Dallas and me.

"Maybe Stevie felt like she needed to go back to Tessa for some reason," Mom says, patting my knee. "But I think you'll find real friendship is stronger than these little speed bumps. And that this is just that—a speed bump."

"But I'm mad at her."

"Anger is usually one of those emotions that's masking another one. Could it be possible you're actually sad because you miss Stevie?" Mom asks.

I stare at her and don't dare tell her she might be right. Instead I hug my knees close to my chest and whisper, "Thanks, Mom."

"All is not lost," she singsongs as she stands up. "You're

young, Jude. You'll have many bumps in life. You'll have many people come into and out of your life too. You just have to decide what's worth fighting for and what's worth letting go."

Or who's worth fighting for and who's worth letting go. I think of Stevie's laughter, her smile, and her kindness. I do think Stevie's worth fighting for, and that idea sparks my determination . . . but also totally terrifies me. What if she really doesn't want to be my friend anymore?

But then another little voice inside me whispers . . . *What have I got to lose by trying?*

CHAPTER 24

I arrive an hour early to the first open meeting of the RSS. Aly's busy working on something at her computer desk and checking out books to people. And Barnaby? He's nowhere to be seen, but he promised he'd be here.

I spend the hour in the meeting room, making up questionnaires to find out what people would like the club to become, and little informational packets to hand out.

I must have rearranged the muffins about a dozen times before there's a knock on the door.

"Hey," Aly says, stepping into the room. "I have two people here from Aberdeen High who would like to know if the Rosedeen Safe Space has started?"

Beaming, I say, "Of course. Bring them in."

I'm sure they aren't expecting a twelve-year-old, but they both give me genuine smiles anyway.

"Hi, I'm Jude. My pronouns are they/them." I hold my hand out to them.

"Clara, she/her," the girl says, her black hair twisted back into space buns. She fidgets with her necklace. She barely reaches the shoulder of her tall, thin friend. "This is Ned. They/them too."

"Cool." I shake Ned's hand, and we sit down at the table. "We have muffins and coffee and tea if you'd like. We'll probably wait until about five after; then we'll start."

"Sounds good," says Ned. "So, you created this group?"

"Yeah," I answer. "With the help of Aly, Barnaby, and my best friend, Dallas. He should be here—Oh! Speak of the devil!"

Dallas laughs in the doorway. "Hey. Sorry I'm a bit late. Mom got home late, and I couldn't leave Aspen—that's my sister—alone. Hi, I'm Dallas."

After Clara and Ned introduce themselves to Dallas, another face shows up at the doorway.

"Excuse me, is this the RSS?"

"Yes, yes! Come in," I say, waving them in. "I'm Jude, and my pronouns are they/them."

"Hi, I'm Rebecca. Um, she/her, I guess." She's a quiet girl, with her hair in a tight ponytail and the most muted clothing I've ever seen a teenager wear. Her skin is paler than mine.

I give my muffin-and-coffee/tea spiel about three more times, and suddenly, I'm sitting at the head of a bustling table. Aly steps in with Barnaby, and they both look pleasantly surprised as they take seats at the other end of the room.

"Hi, everyone, I'm Jude. My pronouns are they/them. I'm queer, nonbinary, and a student at Aberdeen Memorial. With the help of Aly, Barnaby, and my best friend, Dallas, we have created the Rosedeen Safe Space. Welcome to the first meeting."

There are claps, and it finally feels official.

"Our goal is to create a safe space for people to be themselves. Their whole selves. We have some information, an agreement, and a survey. We want to know what *you* would like to see in this club." I take a deep breath, and Dallas gives me a thumbs-up. "Right now, let's go around and anyone who wants to can share a bit about themselves and why they're here."

I start it off with reintroducing myself. "Also I created this club because I saw a need in our community."

"Hi, everybody. I'm Dallas, he/him. I'm gay, and Black—while this is obvious, it's an important part of who I am. I'm excited to be here because there aren't any spaces for me, really."

We turn to look at Clara next. "Hi, I'm Clara, she/her. I'm Korean, demisexual, and Ned's best friend. We were talking about not having many queer friends, so we got excited when we saw the posters."

Ned beams beside her. "Hi, I'm Ned. They/them. I'm non-binary and trans. And I'm biracial—my dad's from Pakistan, and my mom's white."

Aly and Barnaby go next and then we get to Joanna, a teen from Rose Creek High. She's a wheelchair user, and she tells us that she has a hard time making friends. "I'm not queer, though; is it still okay that I'm here?" she asks.

"Do you support queer people?" I ask.

"Of course!"

"Then you're welcome here; it's a safe space for any marginalized people to come together," I explain.

Joanna smiles at me, and then Rebecca shyly introduces herself. A guy named Zack goes next. He doesn't give too many things away but I caught sight of an asexual flag pin on his backpack when he came in.

Dallas nudges me to get my attention and gives me a beaming smile. I can't help but smile back. This is *way* more people than I ever expected.

• • •

"I realized I was demisexual when I had no interest in the most popular kids in our school," Clara tells the group. "But I liked the dorky kid next door. She's *obsessed* with this TV show called *A Little Bit Alexis*. She has all the merch you could imagine. But yeah. She was sort of my clue that I'm more into how someone makes me feel and how I connect with them emotionally."

"So what exactly is demisexuality?" Aly asks kindly.

"It's when you don't experience an initial attraction like

other people do; you have to have an emotional bond of some sort first," Clara explains. "It's on the asexual spectrum."

"Would you consider yourself asexual?" Zack asks. "If it's on the spectrum, I mean? I only ask because I'm asexual and biromantic, and . . . it'd be nice to not feel so alone."

"You're definitely not alone," Clara tells him. "I consider myself part of the asexual community because I'm not allosexual."

"Which is . . . ?" Dallas asks, looking confused. He looks at me, but I shrug. I guess I hadn't gotten to that part in my research.

"When you experience attraction immediately, or at all."

"Huh. So even though I'm gay, I'm also allosexual?"

"Basically. It's how asexual people refer to the sexualities that aren't on the spectrum," Zack explains.

"Can I ask a question?"

We all look at Rebecca. She hasn't said anything until now. I nod. "Of course!"

"Can someone explain the different genders to me?" Rebecca bites down on her lip. "I don't want to be offensive or anything, but I've never met someone who uses they/them pronouns before. I don't really get it."

Ned glances at me, but I motion for them to go ahead. They say, "So, gender is more than a binary of woman and man. If you identify with the gender you're assigned at birth, then you're cisgender—like a cis woman or a cis man. If your assigned gender at birth *isn't* your gender, then you're trans or nonbinary or genderqueer or all of the above."

I jump in. "Yeah, so trans and nonbinary just mean that you aren't cisgender. But while they're identities, they are also umbrella terms."

Barnaby raises an eyebrow. "What does that mean exactly?"

"Basically, they cover a lot of other labels too—for example, genderqueer, genderfluid, agender, bigender, demigender, and so on fall under both the trans and nonbinary umbrellas," Ned explains. "And then the trans umbrella is a little bigger and also includes binary transgender men and transgender women. Gender is pretty fluid for a lot of people."

Rebecca seems to take this all in and gives us the smallest nod. "Thanks for explaining. I don't know what all of those words mean, but . . ."

"*Genderqueer* is like *trans* or *nonbinary* too," Ned says. "It's an umbrella term *and* an identity. Agender is when you don't have a gender—almost like there's a lack of one. Bigender is when you have two or more genders."

"Okay, I think I get it," Rebecca says. "And you use they/them pronouns because . . ."

190

"I use them because they feel the most comfortable," Ned says.

"You know, I've never really thought about my pronouns," Joanna says. "She/her has always felt like me."

"They/them feels like me," I say. "It's whatever you're comfortable with—and people can mix and match their pronouns. I'm not out with my pronouns at school because I didn't feel like having to explain it over and over again."

"It's exhausting," Ned says.

"Um," Clara says, putting up her hand. "Now I have a question . . ."

I lean back in my chair and share a smile with Barnaby. Something good is happening right now, something that I helped create.

• • •

About halfway through the meeting, there's a knock on the door. Ned and Clara are in the middle of a heated but funny debate over a shared memory. Aly gets up to open the door, and in walks Stevie.

I freeze. She freezes.

"Sorry for being late," Stevie says when everyone else looks at her. "I'm Stevie, and I— Maybe I shouldn't be here."

"No," I say, reaching my hand out as if I can stop her from

the other side of the room. "Stay. The Rosedeen Safe Space is open to everyone."

"Are—are you sure?" she asks, her eyes not leaving mine.

"Yes. Please, sit down. Introduce yourself if you want, or just listen. Aly, do you have some more informational stuff?"

"Here, you can have my copy," Dallas says, pushing his papers toward Stevie. We share a quick glance, and I know he's as surprised as I am by Stevie's presence. "I'll get another one from Aly."

"Thank—thank you."

"Do you want to introduce yourself?" Aly asks, blissfully unaware of our history.

Stevie hesitates and then nods. "Hi, I'm Stevie. My pronouns are she/her, and, uh, I think I just want to listen for a bit."

There are some greetings murmured from the group.

"Okay, here's a question!" Ned asks, leaning forward. They obviously sensed some tension and wanted to distract the group. I'm grateful for them. "What's the difference between bisexual and pansexual? Because, like, I identify as bisexual because I like the flag more. But I don't *really* know."

"Well, what are the official definitions?" I ask. "Because it's my understanding that bisexuality is an attraction to two or more genders, and pansexuality is all genders, but regardless of gender."

"Pansexuality includes trans people and bisexuality doesn't," Clara points out . . . incorrectly.

"Bisexuality includes trans people too," says Zack, who has been pretty quiet for a while. "For example, I'm biromantic, and I think Ned is attractive. And I—"

Zack stops talking as Ned dramatically preens like a peacock at the compliment. They flutter their eyelashes at Zack and say, "Exactly, handsome."

Everyone starts to laugh at Ned, and when my eyes meet Stevie's, we're both smiling.

• • •

Somehow the first meeting lasts almost two hours. Everyone has something to say, a truth they've kept to themselves for years. Barnaby's story makes almost everyone cry—he's saved the letters of his long-lost love from when he was in his early twenties.

Dallas admits that with his parents divorcing, he hasn't had any time for crushes on boys; Ned assures him there's always time for boys, and everyone laughs.

Ned manages to keep the mood light, but we do talk about being nonbinary in a small town.

"It's hard. Everyone just *assumes* they know you and your

story," Ned says, shifting in their seat. "They give me a gender that makes sense to them, without really considering how I feel."

"And it's hard to explain that how we feel is totally normal," I say, sighing. "Like, I don't need 'help' or therapy. I know who I am. And who I am doesn't fall in the gender binary."

"Exactly! But if you don't act like they expect you to, or wear what they expect you to wear, you're an outcast."

"Yeah," I say, nodding. It's sweet, having someone who understands exactly how I feel about things.

"I—I—" Stevie starts during a lull near the end of the meeting. All eyes turn to her. "I thought I had a crush on a girl, and that she liked me back, but it turns out she just wants to be friends."

Dallas and I share a look. *Finally*, Stevie feels comfortable sharing her truth with us. This isn't at all how I expected it to go, but I'm glad she's here. I fidget with my hands under the table before I say, "I'm sorry to hear that. Thanks for sharing, even though it sucks, Stevie."

"Yeah. Yeah, it really does."

"Her loss," Clara jumps in. "Besides, you have many more heartbreaks to look forward to."

"Oh, great," Stevie says sarcastically. Everyone laughs, and I swear she looks a little lighter.

CHAPTER 25

I've been thinking about Stevie showing up at the RSS meeting all weekend. I can't get the image of her walking in out of my mind. Did she know the club was my idea? Did she hope to see Dallas and me there?

I tell Dallas to go into our science class without me, and I hover by the door. When Stevie approaches, she smiles, and I smile back.

"There you are!" I hear Tessa's voice from behind me. "I was waiting at your locker for . . ."

But I don't hear what else Tessa says. Instead, I deflate right there. Stevie wasn't smiling at me, was she? She turns her attention toward Tessa, and any hope I have of talking to her goes out the window. I guess she didn't come to the RSS meeting hoping to see me after all.

I slip into the room and give Dallas a shrug when he looks at me questioningly.

Since Stevie's been hanging out with Tessa again, her cell phone goes off *all* the time. It's almost always lit up inside her desk in Mrs. Bayley's class. For a while, Dallas and I used to be the one sending her messages, but now . . .

She left us. I have to remind myself of that.

"Everyone in row A will partner with the person sitting in row B," Mr. Garcia says, pointing at my row and Stevie's row. He continues talking, but I'm stuck on the fact that I'm now partnered with Stevie.

I shoot my hand in the air, feeling Stevie's eyes on me. "Is this a project I should work on with Mr. Middleton?"

Mr. Garcia gives me a small smile. "No, it's not. And just because your hand is raised doesn't mean you can speak out."

"Oh." I pull my hand down. "Sorry."

"It's okay. Just work with Stevie on this assignment, all right?"

Dallas shoots me another look, and for the first time, I can't read his face. Does he want me to play nice? I'm always careful. Is he afraid I'm going to be rude? Because I try not to be.

I give up trying to decipher his expression and push my desk toward Stevie's.

"Can you at least turn your phone off?" I ask when it lights up again. "It's really distracting."

"Oh. Uh, I guess." But she just flips it over inside her desk.

"Okay, then . . . Let's get to work."

I'm opening up my binder when Stevie sets down her pen.

"Can we talk? Like, actually talk?" she says.

"Sure?" I say, shrugging as if it doesn't matter.

It does. I want to know what she has to say.

"I don't want things to be weird between us," Stevie whispers, pushing a piece of paper toward me.

I open it up and read it:

Dear Jude,

I'm sorry for all the pain I have caused you. I wish I could have been a better friend to you like you were to me. I guess I learned how to be a friend from Tessa, and she isn't the best.

Please don't tell anyone my secret. I'm not ready for people to know.

I'm sorry,

Stevie

I scoff after I finish reading it. Then I meet Stevie's worried eyes. "You think I'd tell anyone your secret? I'm not like that, Stevie."

"I—"

"I'm not Tessa." I shake my head and shove the note in my binder. I'll let Dallas read it later. "And for the record, anyone who has to be told not to talk about it . . . probably isn't your greatest ally."

"I know." Stevie fidgets with her hands on top of her desk. "But it's about more than just that. And I just . . . If I could make you understand . . ."

I wait. Is she going to admit the truth? Is she going to acknowledge she dumped Dallas and me? But Stevie doesn't keep talking. She keeps her lips sealed shut. So, I lean forward and force her to look at me.

"Why did you ditch me like that? Like I was *nothing*? Like our friendship didn't matter?"

"I—" Stevie starts, then falters. "I can't tell you."

"You could tell me anything, and I'd believe you. I want an answer." I wave my hand between us. "Just some clarification. Some reason why we're not good enough for you."

"It's not that! It's . . . It's not that," Stevie says. She shifts closer, glancing around to make sure no one's paying attention. Trust me, no one pays me too much attention anyway. "It had nothing to do with you. Can you believe that?"

"Sure it didn't," I say. I want to believe her. Want to trust it had nothing to do with us. I make a snap decision. "Okay. I believe you."

"Just—just like that?" Stevie whispers, eyes wide.

"Yeah," I say, nodding. "Just like that."

"Thank you."

And *that* is why, without thinking, I reach for her hand. I put it in between mine and squeeze. Thankfully, we're at the back of the class, and no one can see us. I let go and pull the assignment closer to us.

Without another word about our friendship—or lack thereof, I guess—I open my textbook and start reading what's required of us.

I feel a buzz in my pocket and pull out my phone, glancing to see Stevie doing the same thing.

> DALLAS (10:34 AM)
> Ummm, are you two okay??
> JUDE (10:35 AM)
> yeah, I think so

I look up to see Dallas looking back at me. He gives me a little thumbs-up, and I respond with a tight smile.

"Do you want to split this into sections?" Stevie asks after she's finished reading the assignment.

"Yeah, sure," I say, distracted.

There's a lot I wish I could say to Stevie, starting with the fact that I miss her. I want to tell her I wish she knew we would never make her jump through hoops to be our friend. And we would love her—all of her—for precisely who she is.

I feel tears sting my eyes, and I dart out of the classroom without warning. I know I should've told Mr. Garcia, but it's hard to ask permission to leave when I don't want anyone to see me cry.

Things feel out of control. Suddenly, I don't know what I'm doing or who I am or what's going on. I run to the single washroom and slip inside when I find it unlocked.

I slide down the wall until I'm sitting on the floor, ignoring how gross it probably is.

The tears come thick and heavy.

"Hey, hey, I'm here," Stevie says. She wraps an arm around my shoulders. I expected Dallas to follow me, but part of me is grateful for Stevie instead.

"How did you find me?" I whisper.

Stevie gives me a look as if it's a silly question. Then she asks, "What's wrong?"

"I don't—I don't know." I collapse into her arms. "Everything was going so well and then it wasn't. You were our friend and then suddenly you weren't. My grandparents still don't know I'm nonbinary. I want to tell them *so* bad, but Mom doesn't think they'll accept me. Not to mention I've been struggling with school because I have ADHD, and sometimes it makes me feel like something's wrong with me. And I *know* that's dumb, because whatever, my brain just doesn't work like everyone else's, and that should be okay. And I didn't even tell you I have ADHD." Stevie jerks back in surprise, but I continue. "Or even my idea for the Rosedeen Safe Space or . . ."

I take a deep breath, but I'm shaking too much to quit crying just yet.

"Hey, hey, it's okay. I'm here." Stevie tugs me a little closer.

Mr. Garcia comes into the hallway and knocks on the door to ask if I'm okay.

"I think Jude needs some time," Stevie says. "Five minutes, and we'll be back in class."

"Okay. Five minutes *tops*," Mr. Garcia says.

We wait a beat until we no longer hear his footsteps in the hallway.

I sniff, lifting my head to look at Stevie. "Thank you."

"It's okay. But you . . . You sound like a lot is going on in your life. I'm sorry I'm part of that."

"Surprise," I say sarcastically. Then I cringe. "Sorry."

"Nah, I deserved it."

We sit in the bathroom for a few minutes while I try to get my crying under control.

"Welcome to the life of Jude," I tell Stevie. "I just want everything to be perfect. Why can't it be perfect?"

"I don't think life works that way, Jude," Stevie says gently. "So, uh, you, um, you have ADHD?"

"Yep."

Stevie stares at me for a moment, and I wonder what she's thinking. She takes a deep breath and then catches me by surprise.

"I have something like that too. It's called dyscalculia."

My eyebrows come together, because I've never heard that word before. But Stevie powers on, her voice small like that day in class when she didn't have the answer for Mrs. Bayley. "I mix up my numbers a lot, because my brain can't read them the same as everyone else's can. My parents hired a private tutor to help me. They didn't want anyone to treat me differently, and they told me to keep it a secret and . . ."

Stevie lets out a breath.

"I guess that's why I haven't wanted anyone to know. But Tessa threatened to tell everyone if I didn't become friends with her again."

I blink before I look at her. "Wait, what? You dumped me and Dallas for Tessa because you're afraid of what people will think if they know you have . . . the numbers thing?"

"Yeah. I know it seems stupid, but . . . if you have ADHD, you must get where I'm coming from, right?"

Do I?

I guess I do.

"It's nothing to be ashamed of."

"It feels like it is. I've spent most of my life try-
ing to compensate for it." Stevie lets out a deep breath.
"Wow, it feels really good to finally tell you that. I miss you,
Jude."

"I miss you too."

"And the RSS is *yours*? I didn't realize that. I saw a flyer
and—" Stevie pauses. "And I realized that if I was scared to
tell people I thought I might be bisexual, at least people there
might understand . . ."

"It's pathetic," I mumble.

"What?"

"It's pathetic that *we* are forced to hide who we are when
they're the ones with the issues," I say, leaning my head back
against the wall. "For the record, I won't tell anyone your
secret. Any of them. I've never been like that. I think Tessa is
totally cruel to use them against you like that."

Stevie snorts. "That's an understatement if I've ever
heard one."

"So, you and Valencia?"

Stevie frowns. "Oh, who knows?"

"That sucks," I say.

"Yeah."

"I miss you, Stevie. I think we could have been grow-old-together friends." I wipe my eyes dry. "I'm sorry Tessa has such control over you. It sucks."

"I'm sorry you're going through so much and I . . . I haven't been there. I suck."

"Maybe a little," I tease. Then we're laughing, and it doesn't feel like the universe is going to explode anymore. It feels like we just saved the world from a huge meteor. Or maybe not, but we're laughing together, and it feels good.

CHAPTER 26

During Monday-night dinner, I can't stop thinking of Stevie. I want to be friends with her forever, just like with Dallas.

And maybe we won't grow old together, but I'll never know if we don't become friends again. In the bathroom, it almost felt like we were.

Someone *might* be able to make the connection between getting everything off my chest and what happens at dinner.

It starts when Pops shouts from the living room. "This Netflix thing is incredible! Did you know about this, **Jude**?"

It takes everything inside me to stop from pointing out he only has it because *I* set it up weeks ago. I cringe as I place some cutlery on the dining room table. I simply call back, "Yep!"

I shoot my mom a look, and she shrugs.

Mom doesn't understand. She's cisgender. Everyone who meets her . . . they all assume her identity correctly. But the world doesn't see *me*. The world can't see me if I'm still standing in the shadows. If I'm still pretending. And maybe to people like Dallas, keeping parts of oneself private works.

But for me, it feels like I'm pretending to be someone else.

I'm going to explode if I can't be myself. My whole self. My nonbinary self.

"Did you know there are thousands of TV shows and movies on here? I can even watch some documentaries!" Pops calls out.

I force myself to take a deep breath.

"When's dinner going to be ready? I'm hungry," Pops says. He doesn't even take his eyes off the TV.

I glance at Nan in the kitchen mashing the potatoes and Mom grabbing something from the oven while I set the table. I don't get how they're so okay with Pops not doing *anything*. Isn't he part of this family too?

"**Jude**."

My grandmother calls me by my deadname for the last time.

It bubbles up within me until I can't control it anymore. Until I can't be who she *thinks* I am. Until I know this is my limit.

I turn to look at her, and something in my face must show the change because she gives me a quizzical look.

"Jude. My name is Jude."

"What?" Nan says, taken aback.

"Kid," my mother says in a warning tone.

This isn't the time, she silently tells me. But it is. It *is* the time.

Sorry if this isn't convenient for you, I want to snap.

Instead, I say louder, "My name is Jude Winters."

"What are you going on about?" Pops says from the living room.

"Maybe instead of sitting on your butt watching TV while everyone else helps get dinner ready, you could come and join us for once and then you'd hear me a little clearer."

"Jude!" my mother hisses. "Quit that, right now."

Pops stands up and walks into the dining room.

"No, Mom. No." I shake my head and set down the cutlery I'm holding. "I'm *tired* of all this. I'm tired of Pops doing nothing while Nan does all the work. I'm tired of Nan apologizing for his behavior in private. I'm tired of being deadnamed and misgendered."

"What has gotten into you, **child**?" Pops asks, red-faced. I bet he's angry. I'm probably the first person to call him out on his laziness. "Betty, do something about this."

Nan looks a little lost.

My mom holds up her hands. "I think Jude is trying to tell you something important."

"What?" Pops demands, staring me down. "You think you're tough enough to disrespect me like that in my own home?"

"Yeah, well, you disrespected Nan. You should be helping her, not sitting there doing nothing."

"I did my time. I work hard every darn day to make sure my family is taken care of. I'll do as I please."

"Doesn't Nan work hard too?" I ask, looking over at her. She seems smaller somehow, staring at me like she's only just seen me for the first time. "And that's not what I'm trying to tell you!"

My mom comes over to put her hands on my shoulders.

"My name is Jude. And I'm telling you that I'm nonbinary. I'm not a girl. I'm not a boy. I'm nonbinary. My pronouns are they/them."

"What?" Pops asks, rolling his eyes. "What are you talking about?"

"If you'd *listen*, I'm telling you." I lean into my mom's grip. "My name is Jude."

"Like hell it is! You will not disrespect your mother's choice of a name like this. She chose your name, and you will keep it."

I feel the tears coming, but I don't know what else to say.

"Why do you kids need to label everything anyway?" he demands.

Because it gives me a community. A place where I belong. Because in all these confusing feelings, I am not alone. I am not alone, and that is a relief in this big world.

"Dear, why don't you go back to Netflix? I'll talk to . . . *Jude* here," Nan says, eyeing Pops. He grumbles and storms into the living room. Nan sits down at the table, asking me politely to join her. "Can you explain this to me?"

"I'm trying," I whisper. The tears are hitting my eyes now, so I turn into my mother's arms. "Mom?"

I don't even have to say the words, and she knows I need her help.

We sit down at the table. It's a long discussion, and Nan tries to be supportive. At one point, she says, "I'll do my best, but I don't know if I'll ever get the hang of *they/them*. It's the grammar for me, really. It makes no sense."

"Actually," I say sniffling, "Jane Austen used they and them pronouns to describe singular people in the early 1800s."

"Oh?"

"And you already do use them," I explain. "Pretend you're at a party and someone leaves their umbrella. You don't know the owner of it, right? It could be a girl, a boy, or a nonbinary person."

"Okay," Nan says, nodding.

"So, what would you say to your friend? You wouldn't say, 'Someone forgot his or her umbrella.' You'd say, 'Someone forgot *their* umbrella.' And just like that, you've used *they* as a singular pronoun."

"This is important to you, isn't it?" Nan asks.

"Yes. It's who I *am*. Don't you want to know who I am? Don't you want to love me for who I am?"

"Yes, I do. I'll talk to Pops about it. See if we can't work on his stubbornness. He'll come around, just like he did with Netflix." Nan reaches out and puts her hand on mine. "I love you, Jude."

"Love you too," I say, and just like her, I pretend I didn't call my grandfather out for being lazy.

Maybe it's best not to rock the boat *too much*.

• • •

"So, kid, want to tell me what that was all about?" Mom asks when we get into the car. "Because I did *not* see that coming."

I fidget with my rusty-orange sweater before saying, "I can't seem to control my feelings anymore. I feel like a ticking time bomb, just ready to go off at any time."

"Ah, I remember that age. It'll get easier. So, how do you feel now?"

"Okay, I guess? I'm sorry about all that."

"Don't be. I'm sorry I ever suggested you keep it from them," Mom says. She reaches over and gives my hand a squeeze. "Although, a warning the next time you're going to yell at your grandparents would be nice."

I wince. "Sorry. I just . . . I didn't want to pretend

anymore." I take a deep breath. "I'm done pretending. I think . . . I think I just want to be myself from now on."

"Okay. I'm excited for the world to see how special you are."

"I'm mad at you too, you know."

Mom glances at me. "Oh?"

"You didn't want me to tell them." I tug on the sleeve of my shirt. "I don't think that was very nice of you."

"Oh, honey, I just didn't want to see you get hurt."

"But I was already hurting."

I think a light bulb goes off in that moment. Her lips part and close twice before she settles on a soft "I'm so sorry. I guess I thought I was protecting you. Are we going to be okay?"

I give her a small smile and ask, "Depends. Am I grounded for yelling at them?"

"Nah. This is your one freebie. Just don't do it again."

"Then we're okay."

CHAPTER 27

"I came out to my grandparents," I tell the room at the second RSS meeting. I'm nervous and unsure what else to say, but this feels right. It feels good to tell these people, people who will understand.

Ned whistles. "I haven't even done that. Good for you."

"What do you mean?" I ask, frowning. "I thought you were out to everyone."

"Everyone except my family. My mom knows, and she's cool with it, but . . . it's hard telling everyone you know that the image they had of you is all wrong." Ned shrugs; then they give me an encouraging smile. "You are one brave kid. I hope you know that."

I don't feel very brave. I squirm slightly in my chair, and Dallas squeezes my hand. Stevie isn't here tonight, and I wonder why. I think it's a bit easier with her around, frankly.

"Do you want to talk about it some more?" Barnaby asks.

I shrug.

"That's okay. Remember, sharing is encouraged but not

required," Aly says. Her warm smile reminds me a bit of Stevie.

I glance at Dallas. "I guess I was wishing for *more*. More understanding. More willingness to listen. More . . . just . . . more."

"How did they react?" Clara asks, looking at me curiously. Her eyes are really big, so it feels like I'm under a microscope.

"I don't know. Pops yelled a lot. Said I should respect my mother's choice of name and . . ." I trail off, flinching as the memory rushes back to me. Dallas squeezes my hand again.

"And it didn't go well," Dallas continues for me. "They weren't very open."

"Well, Nan at least *tried* by talking to me about it," I correct.

"At least you did it," Ned points out. "And that's courageous as hell, kid."

I shrug again. Is it brave to come out? I only wanted people to view me *as me*. Not this idea they have of me in their heads. I want to grow up and be me. I don't want to be stuck in this pinhole version of myself when there's so much more to me than that.

Like starting this club. Can anyone see how awesome that is? Or reaching out to someone I wouldn't otherwise talk to when they needed a friend. Holding Dallas's hand when he gets scared. Standing up for what's right. Trying to balance my identity and my mother's worries.

Coming out is just one piece of me—one piece of my story. I don't want it to be my whole identity.

Yes, being nonbinary is important to me. I am neither girl nor boy. I do not fit into those categories, that binary. But I also don't think that being nonbinary is all I am . . .

"Maybe it's brave," I whisper. "Or stupid. I don't know. But I'm . . . I'm not *just* nonbinary. I'm smart. I work hard. I'm kind. I want to make the world a better place. And I . . . I'm a good friend."

"The best," Dallas says, grinning.

"And I am the same person I was before I came out to them." Tears fill my eyes. "Why can't they see that? All the things they loved about me before I came out . . . they're still there. Nan said that she still loved me, but Pops said nothing . . . Why is it so hard to love me now?"

Dallas immediately wraps his arms around me, hugging me for dear life. I cling to him. Ned and Clara join us. Then Barnaby, Aly, and Zack. And Rebecca. And then we shuffle over to include Joanna. Suddenly, I'm in the middle of the biggest group hug.

"You're not hard to love," Ned whispers. They brush

some of my hair from my face, just like Dallas usually does. "They're wrong if they think that."

The tears pour out of me, almost uncontrollably. And I don't know if I'm sad that my pops reacted so weirdly, as if I was someone else, or if I'm happy that I've found a place where I can be as honest as possible.

"Okay, okay, I can't breathe!" I say, and everyone starts to pull away. But Dallas slips his hand right back into mine and squeezes. I laugh and brush the tears away. "Thank you."

"You're one of the most incredible people I've ever met," Aly announces with kindness dancing in her eyes. "You've done something really cool here, Jude."

"Yeah," I whisper, looking around at the other club members. "I have."

• • •

"I guess I feel like it was a long time coming, you know," Rebecca says, tugging at the sleeves of her shirt. "When my parents saw me kissing a girl, they lost their cool. First, they yelled at me; then they said nothing and acted as if it didn't happen."

I glance around the group. Everyone wears an empathetic expression of some kind. Right now, it's Rebecca's turn to share, and no one wants to interrupt. She pushes a piece of hair from her face and continues.

"I think the screaming was preferable," Rebecca admits. "At least then I existed to them. But now . . . Well, I'm living with a friend's family. It's okay, and they've been nothing but kind to me, but they . . . They don't really get what it's like. And I don't want to overstay or . . ."

She squeezes her eyes shut. I want to reach across the table to grab her hand, but I can't. Instead I quietly say, "It's better to be safe than sorry."

Rebecca looks up at me and gives me a sad smile that doesn't reach her eyes. "Yeah. I guess."

"If you ever need another place to crash, let me know," Ned offers. "My parents renovated our garage into a bedroom for my older brother, but he's not living there anymore. I would've moved into it, but I didn't see the point since I'm leaving for school in a year."

Rebecca's eyes light up. "Really?"

"Really. I doubt my parents would mind. My dad's a trucker, so he's not really home that often anyway. And my mom is totally cool with the queer stuff . . ." Ned pauses before adding, "Not that you'd have to tell her. I'm sure I could set something up."

"I'd—I'd really appreciate that. I could pay rent! I have a part-time job and—"

"I doubt my parents would take your money," Ned says,

with that easygoing smile of theirs. "But I'll mention it."

"Thank you," Rebecca whispers.

I look at Dallas, and I know we're thinking the same thing: how we're incredibly lucky to have some family that love us. Even if Mom didn't react the way I wanted her to the first time, and even if my grand-ghosts never understand me, it could've been *a lot* worse. I am loved. By Mom, by Dallas, and I dare say . . . I'm even loved by Stevie.

Rebecca and Ned quietly discuss living arrangements, and I meet Barnaby's eyes. He gives me one simple nod, and I know. I know that none of this would've been possible without the Rosedeen Safe Space.

• • •

"I still have goose bumps," Dallas tells me as we take the long walk home from the meeting an hour and a half later. It's not supposed to last that long, but like the first meeting, we needed the extra time. He elbows me gently. "You never hear people saying those kinds of things about themselves. But I'm glad you see why you're so awesome, Jude."

I smile, exhausted but happy. "Thanks, Dal."

"You're right, though." Dallas hooks his arm in mine. He's been more touchy-feely lately, but I don't mind. I think touch is my love language—Joanna shared love languages with the group tonight after Rebecca finished talking.

"I'm glad you know you're so much more than being non-binary. I don't know if your gender will change how your grandparents view you, but if it does, they're dumb." Dallas kicks a rock ahead of us, and I kick it next. "You're the best friend in the world."

"I try." But then the moment feels heavier than usual, so I add, "I'll always try, Dallas. Even when we're old and have wrinkles like Barnaby."

He laughs, and it's the best sound I've heard all day.

CHAPTER 28

Soon, a month has passed since the night at my grandparents' house. I haven't been over for Monday-night dinner since. Mom has gone twice, but she says Pops is still expecting an apology from me.

"Nan is trying," she promises. "She even bought a book about pronouns and gender."

I haven't talked much to Stevie, just here and there between classes. She texts me sometimes, but I don't know how to respond. I want her to be my friend again, to hang out with Dallas and me, but I'm still hurt. And she wants it to be on the downlow, because she's not ready for people to know about her learning disability. I think her parents put a lot of pressure on her to be a perfect student. Plus, it takes me a while to process my emotions, and that's okay.

Dallas and I are having a sleepover at his dad's new house—his dad has been much happier living on his own; he doesn't even yell anymore. He rented a house a few blocks away so that it isn't too far from Dallas's mom's house. It's the first time I've ever been inside, and it's much smaller. But

Dallas has his own room, so I guess being the only boy in a big family has some perks.

We're in the living room when Jersey pokes her head in. "Hey, Jude. When's your next meeting for the RSS?"

"We meet twice a month. The first and third Friday," I answer. "Are you thinking of joining us?"

"Nah, but I have a friend who is questioning. Think they'd be okay to join you once or twice, even if they don't know?"

"Absolutely! You could come to support them if you want," I tell her, beaming. I look at Dallas, and his eyes are shining. "How did you hear about it?"

"I saw a flyer in Dallas's room," Jersey says, "and I've overheard you talking about it."

"Oh." I look at Dallas, eyes wide.

"I came out to them last week," Dallas says. "Just Aspen and Jersey. And Paris. I haven't figured out how to tell Brooklyn or Holland."

"What?! How did you not tell me?" I smack him gently on the knee.

"Sorry! We've just been . . ." Dallas waves his arms around.

I get it. We've been quieter than usual. Dallas's focus has been on moving and getting new things for his dad's place. I've been trying to keep my world relatively calm, feeling lighter than I have in a long time. And we're both missing Stevie. It's funny how she was only a friend for a fleeting period of time, but she managed to have such an impact on us.

"Anyway, I'll let them know. Thanks." Jersey pauses before adding, "Also, Paris told Brooklyn, who told Holland. So the sisters all know. Hope that's okay, Dallas."

"Oh!" Dallas gives her a thumbs-up. "Yeah, that's easy. They took it okay?"

"It's not theirs to take," Jersey says, rolling her eyes. "It's their issue if they need time to process or whatever, but it's not their news to take. Does that make sense? It's yours to give. And only when you want to. Paris just thought Brooklyn already knew."

"Uh . . ." I start.

"I'm cool with it," Dallas continues. "Jude, you okay?"

"I'm great." I jump up and run toward Jersey. I wrap my arms around her. "Thank you."

"What's going on?" Aspen asks, coming back into the living room with some popcorn. She gives me a weird look. "Why are you . . . like that?"

"Because," I say, wrapping an arm around her shoulders dramatically, "I'm in a good mood. Can I have some popcorn?"

"If you must."

· · ·

I'm crawling into Dallas's bed when he shoves my shoulder. "Whoa, whoa, stay on your side."

"I am!"

"No, you're definitely inching onto my side," Dallas grumbles.

We situate ourselves, and then I lean my head back, staring up at his ceiling. "I like your other ceiling better."

"Yeah. It has the glow-in-the-dark stuff all over it," Dallas points out. "This ceiling is boring."

"Yeah."

We sit in silence for a little longer until I whisper, "I know why Stevie went back to Tessa."

"What?" Dallas sits upright. "How long have you known?"

"A while. I . . . I didn't think I should say anything, but . . . I really miss her. Don't you?" I ask, my voice barely above a hushed whisper.

"Of course. What's the deal? What happened?"

"Tessa," I say, and sigh heavily. I sit up and cross my legs. "She has a secret on Stevie that Stevie doesn't want to get out."

"Being queer?"

"Not just that, but also something else. I don't know if I should say. I think Tessa stopped being friends with Stevie because of her queerness, and now she's using another secret to reel her back in. But it's been long enough. I think it's time to get our friend back."

"Okay," Dallas says, nodding. "But . . . How?"

I look up at the ceiling, as if an answer will come to me suddenly. I don't know how, but I think it starts with a text.

JUDE (9:46 PM)
hey, this is crazy, but here's my number so call me maybe

"Did you just use Carly Rae Jepsen to get our friend back? That's your big idea?" Dallas asks, but he's smiling. And that's all that matters. "Jude, you're ridiculous."

"I know."

Then we burst into laughter and settle into bed.

• • •

She calls at 7:13 a.m. I groan and throw my pillow over my face as Dallas nudges me.

"Stevie," he says, his voice muffled.

I reach for my phone, my face squashed against the mattress, and snag it. I wish I could say I was graceful and answered immediately. Instead, I drop my phone and have to fish around for it. By the time I get it to my ear, I've missed the call.

"Darn it," I mutter, calling back. I bring the phone to my ear and close my eyes.

"Hello?"

"You suck," I mumble. "It's *so* early."

Stevie's laughter is familiar, safe, and good. I flush with delight and sit up.

"I'll have you know I've been awake for the last hour. I've been itching to call you maybe."

I laugh. "It was good, wasn't it?"

"It's because I was obsessed with her new song, isn't it?"

"Yep."

Dallas gives me a thumbs-up and yawns. "Hey, Stevie. I'm here too."

"Dallas! Hi." Stevie pauses before asking, "Is everything okay?"

"Well, we had a question for you. Please be as honest as possible," I say. "But do you really want to be friends with Tessa?"

"Um." There's a long pause, and I hush Dallas when he tries to say something to fill the silence. Finally, Stevie says, "No, not really. I always have to be . . . *on*. With you two, it was so easy."

"And the secret you told me? The one you don't want to get out?" I ask. "Do you still want to keep it a secret?"

"Yeah, but not from Dallas." Stevie sniffs before taking a deep breath and explains, "I have a learning disability."

"Like Jude's ADHD?" Dallas asks.

"Sort of. It's called dyscalculia. I can't—See, the thing is . . . Numbers are all messed up for me. I struggle a lot with number stuff." Stevie pauses.

"Oh, that must make math hard!" Dallas says.

Stevie lets out a small laugh. "Yeah. Yeah, it really does. But my parents hired a private tutor so I wouldn't fall behind in school—they're sort of embarrassed by it. They told me not to tell anyone."

"Why? Were they afraid you'd get made fun of?" Dallas asks.

"I think so. Or that people would judge us." Stevie sounds like she's frowning.

"It's not a big deal," I say to her. "I promise. Everyone gets help for stuff all the time. I thought I could manage things on my own, but I've realized that leaning on people and asking for help is okay."

"Yeah?"

"Yeah. You can't do *everything* on your own." We can hear her making some noise in the background. Stevie says, "But I still don't want everyone to know."

"So, we say nothing. Let the rumors fly. We make a big

deal about me going to Mr. Middleton for ADHD, and . . ." I shrug at Dallas. "And never confirm or deny your learning disability. Let people think what they think."

"I'm not like you, Jude. I can't just let people think what they think."

"Why not?"

"Because! What if they think awful things about me?"

"Do *you* think you're awful? Or broken?" I ask, scrunching my eyebrows together.

"No, but . . . I'm not normal."

"Who is?" I demand. "No one's normal, Stevie. We all have our things. But I came out to my grandparents and—"

"You did?" Stevie interrupts.

"I did. And it wasn't the worst thing in the world. It sucked, but it wasn't the worst. And if I can do that, you can let some people think what they want to think. You're never going to change their minds anyway." I take a breath and go in for the final note. "We miss you, Stevie. Be our friend."

"Just like that?" she says, and I can hear a smile in her voice.

"Just like that," I promise. I wait a beat, then ask, "So, did I pass?"

Hearing Stevie's unfiltered laughter come through the phone is incredible. I grab Dallas's hand, and we wait anxiously. Then Stevie says, "A wise person once told me there are no tests in friendship. It's not a quiz you pass. Some things are just like that."

"Wait, so after *all* that, you're just going to be friends with us again?" Dallas asks.

"I was never *not* your friend. Not truly." Stevie lets out a deep breath. "You'll have my back?"

"Always," Dallas says.

"Until we're old, baby!" I shout, and then the three of us dissolve into giggles. Some things are worth fighting for.

CHAPTER 29

At school on Monday, I run up to Stevie's locker. I put my hands over her eyes and say, "Guess who?"

"Jude, I know it's you," Stevie says, giggling. She turns around and gives me a bright, warm smile. "Hi."

"Hi. I have a gift for you." I reach into my pocket and hand it over.

She looks down into her palm. "A horse eraser?"

"Just as a joke," I answer. "I found it in my school stuff from last year. Thought you'd like it."

"Oh my god," Stevie says, shaking her head. She thumbs it around in her hand before looking up at me. "Thanks, Jude."

"You don't just have to face your fears, you can *erase* your fears!"

Stevie groans harder than I expect at my pun.

"How is the horse thing?" I whisper.

"Still going. She wants to take me to the stables now!" Stevie whispers back.

I neigh like a horse, and Stevie playfully shoves me, but there's a smile on her face that's impossible to miss.

. . .

"You're *sure* she won't come in here?" Dallas asks for the third time since we all met up at my locker. He's on the lookout for Tessa, afraid we're going to spark her wrath. He doesn't want to deal with her today, and frankly, neither do I.

I glance at Stevie, who nods and pops her hood up. "She won't, but just in case."

"It's not always going to be like this, right?" I ask. My leg is shaking so hard I hit the table. "Oof."

"Jeez, you two. I thought you wanted to spend lunch together," Stevie says, smiling. "Trust me, Tessa isn't going to come into the school library. It's not her scene unless she absolutely has to. But even then . . . I've never seen her here."

"Cool, cool, cool," Dallas says. "I still feel like she's going to appear out of nowhere and curse us to the underworld or something."

I smile and tousle my hair before opening my lunch. "So, she's still blackmailing you?"

Stevie nods. "All because I didn't want to cheat on a test as one of her friendship tests. How dumb is that—"

"Wait. *What?*" I say at the same time that Dallas says, "Cheating on a test?"

"Yeah, but I thought you knew that," Stevie says,

looking between us. Her eyes land on mine. "You said—"

"I thought she was blackmailing you for being queer," I whisper, horrified.

Stevie's eyes grow wide. "Oh my god!"

"Yeah, definitely had some miscommunication there. That was the rumor going around when Tessa first unfriended you."

"Well, it's not true! I didn't want to let Tessa cheat off me for Mr. Garcia's science test, so she kicked me out. Tessa would *never* use someone's sexuality against them. She was the one who suggested I join the RSS in the first place. We grabbed one of the posters by the movie theater. Plus, I think there might be something going on with her and Valencia."

"Whoa, whoa. So much information to process in a short time," I say before I start to laugh quietly. "Wow, we sure got that wrong. Tessa and Valencia . . . ?"

"Yeah. After I spent so much time with you two, she and Tessa got close. I'm not really sure if they're more than friends, but I know you two won't tell anyone," Stevie explains. "You have to promise, though."

"Pinkie swear," Dallas and I say in unison, holding out our pinkies.

"That's not what I was expecting to hear," I say, shaking my head as my cell phone buzzes. I pull it out of my pocket and freeze.

MOM (11:13 AM)

Head's up—we're going to Nan and Pops' tonight. They're

trying, Jude. They love you.

JUDE (11:14 AM)

nooooooooooooooooooooo please no

MOM (11:14 AM)

Don't worry—if they act up, we'll leave immediately. Just

try? For me?

JUDE (11:14 AM)

Okay, for you

"Ugggggggggh."

"What was that noise for?" Dallas asks. When I lift my head from my phone, they're both staring at me.

I show them the text messages. "I have to go to dinner tonight."

"Nooo," Dallas says, shaking his head. "That sucks."

"After how he treated you? Rude. But I guess . . ." Stevie sighs and scrunches her nose. "I guess it's good that your nan is trying."

"Ugh," I repeat.

I put my head in my hands and close my eyes.

• • •

After lunch, Dallas goes to the washroom, saluting as we part, and Stevie walks with me to my locker. We hover beside it for a few moments before I realize she's trying to muster the courage to say something. Bracing myself mentally, I take a breath and wait. I don't want to rush her.

Finally, she speaks. "Jude, can I ask you something?"

"Always," I reply. I glance around for Tessa, but Stevie doesn't seem too concerned about being caught together. She tucks a piece of her fallen hair behind her ear and bites her bottom lip. I gently put my hand on her arm. "What's up?"

"I don't get why you aren't angrier at me." Her eyebrows come together, and she lets out a small huff of air. "I treated you so badly, and I—"

"Hey," I say before she works herself into a panic. I squeeze her arm, rubbing my thumb in small circles. "Stevie, I *was* angry at you. I was furious. I didn't understand why or how you could ditch us after we were your friends when you needed it most."

Stevie pulls her arm away to hug herself. Her eyes are wide and her lips part, but she doesn't say anything.

"But I also just missed you a lot," I tell her honestly. "I guess it doesn't seem like such a big deal anymore, because

I'd rather have you in my life than not at all. Dallas kind of helped me understand that."

"And your anger?"

"It's just . . ." I shrug. "Gone? I don't know. Besides, it's not like you were doing it on purpose. You were manipulated."

"But you didn't know that!"

"But I do *now*." I give her a small smile. "What kind of person would I be if I didn't change my mind when presented with new information?"

"A crappy one," she says, her lips twitching into a smile. "I didn't let Tessa say anything bad about you, you know."

And somehow, I do know.

"You can do anything," Stevie decides, nodding. "And you can get through this dinner with your grandparents."

I'd almost forgotten. I cringe and groan too loudly. "Ugh, this is going to be the worst."

But maybe, just maybe, it won't be.

CHAPTER 30

"The second they do *anything*, we'll leave."

"Yeah," I say, closing my eyes and pressing my head against the car window. "I know. You've said that twice already. I'm just . . ."

I trail off, and Mom waits patiently for me to finish. It rushes out of me all at once: "What if they don't love me?"

"They love you, and they'll love you no matter what."

"You don't know that."

"I *do* know that, because, Jude, I am so proud of you. Look at everything you are, and everything you've accomplished. Creating a safe-space club for people of all ages? Only my kid could pull off something so incredible, all while juggling school and ADHD," she tells me.

"But—" I start and stop. "Mom, I thought you hated the RSS. You never really asked me about it."

"No. I hated that your grades were slipping and you weren't able to focus on school, but you've become so much happier because of it. So self-assured. It's a great thing you've created, Jude." She wipes my cheek when we come to a stop sign. I guess a tear had fallen. "I'm proud of you. Starting up again with Mr. Middleton wasn't easy, but you did it. I love you, kid."

In this moment, I know two things: First, my mother loves me. No qualifier. No *no matter what*, as if I'm broken somehow and she loves me despite it. She loves me. All of me. Second, I'm going to be okay. I have my mother and my friends, and right now, that's everything I've ever needed.

I lean into her. "Love you, Mom."

"Love you too, kid. Love you too."

On that note, we fall into silence. The car ride has been intense, but I think my mom understands how important this dinner is.

When we pull into the driveway, I'm shaking. I don't know what this means. I don't know how long I'll be able to stay.

Nan opens the door before we get a chance to knock.

"Jude! I'm so happy to see you. Come here, my child." And Nan wraps her arms around me, holding me close. I wish I could stop shaking, but even when she smiles brightly at me, my hands tremble.

"Hi."

"Come in, come in," she says. "Earl, Jude is here."

She isn't even hesitating with my name. There's no

stammer, no stutter, nothing. And she's used it twice already. What is happening?

"Hey, kiddo." Pops is standing in the dining room putting some plates on the table. *Kiddo? Setting the table? What alternate universe have I entered?* Then Pops says, "Before dinner, Nan and I were wondering if we could talk."

"Uh, sure," I manage. He doesn't seem mad at me.

He finishes up with the plates, and the four of us sit down in the living room. I glance at my mom, unsure and so darn hopeful.

Pops clears his throat. "I owe you an apology, Jude. I don't agree with *how* you told me your feelings, but I do recognize that I had fallen into some old habits."

"Okay," I breathe. My chest is so tight. "Sorry about how I blew up."

"Nan bought some books, so we've been reading a lot. We've also watched some TV shows and movies with nonbinary people in them. There's not a whole lot out there, huh?" he says, and I nod. "And I can understand why me sitting around doing nothing could have made you angry. It was very—Betty, what's the word?"

"Patriarchal."

"Right. Patriarchal. And it was . . ."

"It was unfair," Nan says, reaching out to grab Pops's

hands. "We have some old-fashioned habits. And we can see now how that must have been hard and confusing for you, especially when they are based on genders you don't fit into."

I didn't realize that.

I didn't know.

But now I'm starting to breathe again. I'm trying to hold it together, but I've never seen my grandparents like this. They're shy, awkward, unsure, and it feels like they've practiced this little speech.

"We're going to do better. And you'll have to excuse us. They/them pronouns are new to us," Nan continues. She reaches out and puts a hand on my knee. "But I promise you, we're going to try our absolute best. We love you, Jude. No matter what."

There it is again. The *no matter what*. But this time, I don't doubt it. I rush forward, wrapping my arms around both of them.

Relief washes over me. I thought this night would be terrible. That I would go home in tears. Instead, I'm crying, but I think they're happy tears.

"Thank you. Thank you so much."

"We love you, Jude," my grandfather says, cupping my face in one of his weathered hands. "I'm sorry I ever let you doubt that. We've been doing our research, and we're trying."

"That's all I ever wanted," I whisper. I squeeze them tight again before I pull back to wipe away my tears. I rush over to my mother and hug her too. She made this happen. I know she did.

"Whew," Nan says.

"Let's eat," Mom adds.

"Oh! The bread!" Pops shouts suddenly. He jumps up and hurries into the kitchen. I look at my mom and Nan, and we share bewildered looks.

"He's going to try harder to blur the gender roles." Nan grins. "This is great for me, but also, he wants me to get into sports. How on earth am I supposed to care about people playing games?"

"Who knows?" Mom says. "But I appreciate you making the effort."

"Sports are something you either love or hate," I point out. "But, hey, maybe this means you could go out to a game together."

"A date night!" Nan claps her hands. "I like that. I could always go for a sausage from the stadium. They have the best ones downtown."

"It's hardly a stadium, though," I say.

"It's the closest thing we've got."

I realize suddenly that everything is different and the

same. Pops shouts for my help in the kitchen, and we spend the night laughing at his disaster of a meal. Even so, he doesn't make any jokes about how it should stay Nan's job; instead, he asks if she'll help him with the roast next week.

"I'll do better," he promises, and I believe him.

Maybe the world doesn't need saving. Maybe change starts right here, with family, and maybe that's enough. Because right now? Right now, I feel as though everything is going to be okay.

At the end of the night, I shoot a text to my group chat with Dallas and Stevie.

JUDE (8:46 PM)
They called me Jude forty-nine times. Messed up my pronouns twice. Got them right eighteen times

All the heart emojis I receive back echo the love I feel pooling inside me, warm and bright, and full of potential.

EPILOGUE

Some things I'm learning and some things I know for sure: I think life is messy, and no one really knows what they're doing. I'm pretty sure things are going to be a little awkward with my grandparents for a while. But Nan took me shopping and bought me a new outfit. She even acknowledged how hard it must be to find clothes when they're split into women's and men's sections. And then she found a really nice cardigan in the men's section of Value Village and decided to buy it for herself. It was a good moment, and it gave me even more hope for our future.

The Rosedeen Safe Space has grown into something bigger than me, and I love that. People come and go these days, but the core group remains the same. We're all still learning so much about one another, and we've even scheduled a Queer History Trivia Night. But the biggest surprise was when Tessa showed up to a meeting. She actually pulled Stevie, Dallas, and me aside during a break and apologized for how she treated us. Dallas thinks Tessa apologized because she wanted to join the RSS, but I think she missed her friend.

And to be honest, I don't really think I'll ever fully understand what happened between Stevie and Tessa, but I don't think it's up to me to understand.

Things with Dallas's family are better too. His parents are getting along for the first time in years. His mom hums while she makes dinner now. And his dad surprised him with a newer, fancier iPod, but he still uses the one from his sister. I even caught Dallas singing Britney Spears the other day, and that's how you *know* he's happy.

•   •   •

Dallas and I are walking to class a few weeks after Tessa's big apology. Yesterday she and Valencia even came over and chatted with us at lunch. I'm still not sure whether we can fully trust her, so we'll see how it goes, but I'm willing to at least give her a chance.

We're about to go into English when Dallas asks, "Did you ever picture us like this? Friends with Stevie? Not enemies with Tessa? Running an all-ages safe-space club?"

"Sort of," I say. "But I couldn't have seen the Tessa stuff coming. And I didn't see the RSS growing as much as it has. Did I tell you Aly's putting in a changing room downstairs so trans and unhoused people can browse donations and take the clothes they need? She officially got it approved by the board."

"Whoa. You're really changing the world, Jude. Do you realize that?" Dallas asks, teasing me. He gently nudges me and adds, *Jude Saves the World*. That's what you should call your autobiography."

"Hey, who knows? Maybe I will."

"What, save the world or name your book?"

"Both?"

We laugh and enter Mrs. Bayley's classroom. She gives me a note, and I head to Mr. Middleton's office to work on our new assignment. There's a bounce in my step, because this project is something I'm passionate about. What is it? To write a creative story with yourself as the main character going on a life-changing journey. I can't wait to tell the truth of my story.

So, without further ado . . .

AUTHOR'S NOTE

Jude Saves the World is both the story of my soul and an apology to my twelve-year-old self.

When I was twelve, I had no idea that anything beyond the gender binary existed. *Nonbinary, transgender, bisexual,* and *queer* were not words that were whispered between kids like *gay* and *lesbian* were. All I knew about was two genders, never a rainbow, never a mixture of all the above, never none of the above. I struggled for years, fluctuating between wearing dresses and feeling like I was playing a part and joining auto class in high school to do the things boys were doing. No matter what I did, I was always on the outside looking in, wondering where I fit.

I didn't fit with the girls, and I didn't fit with the boys, and I didn't fit anywhere. When I met someone who was nonbinary for the first time, it felt like my world went from black-and-white to thousands and millions of different colors splashing everywhere. Suddenly, I made sense. I now understood I didn't belong in the boxes society had built for me, and I could finally exhale.

This book is dedicated to the kid in me who struggled for

so long. I gave Jude my identities: queer, bisexual, nonbinary, trans, and neurodivergent. But I did not give Jude a struggle over who they are, because this is their gift from me: They know. They know who they are, but they don't know how to tell the world, and that's where they stumble. Because had someone given me the representation that I so, so needed as a kid, had someone sat me down and taught me that there's a whole rainbow of colors out there, I would've known.

Jude's assigned gender at birth and deadname are never revealed, because I want you to see through Jude's eyes. They aren't a girl or a boy. They're just Jude.

To my young trans, nonbinary, and queer readers, I hope that you find pieces of yourself within *Jude Saves the World*. I wish you all the unconditional love and strength in the world. I hope you feel seen by the queer characters in Jude's story, and you trust you are not alone in those big, confusing, messy feelings. You matter to this world. You are *not* disposable.

Finally, *Jude Saves the World* has many different coming-out stories, including those of Jude, Dallas, Stevie, and the other members of the RSS. It was important to me to show that there's no one way to come out, and that queer people rarely come out just once. Instead, we have to come out over and over again during all stages of life. There can be devastating, heartbreaking, gut-wrenching coming out stories, but

I never wanted Jude's to be one of them. To me, *Jude Saves the World* isn't about coming out. It's about having a fierce sense of self, knowing what you deserve, and standing up for yourself even when it's hard. To me, Jude's story was a way to show that even the best, most well-meaning people can make mistakes and hurt us, and that educating ourselves on lives that are different than our own is important. To me, Jude is the hero I needed when I was twelve years old.

Jude Saves the World saved me. I hope it saved a little piece of you too.

With love,
Ronnie

QUEER GLOSSARY

This glossary is intended to introduce you to language that queer people and their allies often use, but it is not exhaustive by any means. These are basic definitions, and gender and sexuality can be complex, nuanced, and fluid. We have designed this glossary to give you starting places rather than rules, as people may experience or understand these terms differently than what we've included here. More than anything, it's important to respect people's personal choices, language, and identities.

This glossary was made in 2022 with careful consideration, love, and compassion. However, language can also change over time, and if any of these terms become outdated, we will strive to change with them.

GENDER

Agender: describes a person who does not have or experience a gender

Assigned gender at birth: the gender someone is given

when they are born; this may or may not match their gender identity

Bigender: describes a person who is two or more genders (e.g., girl, boy, and/or nonbinary, etc.)

Chosen name: the name a trans person decides to use instead of their birth name

Cisgender: describes a person whose gender matches their assigned gender at birth; sometimes shortened to *cis*

Coming out: describes someone who is not cisgender voluntarily sharing their gender identity; can also be used in reference to sexuality (see below)

Deadname: the birth name given to a trans person that they have chosen to no longer use; can also be used as a verb (e.g., to deadname someone)

Demigender: describes a person who tends to be one gender over others, but is not wholly cisgender (e.g., demigirl, demiboy, deminonbinary, etc.)

Gender binary: a system that views people as only being either girls or boys

Gender expression: how someone presents themselves to the world (e.g., through their clothing or hair); one's gender expression may not represent their gender identity

Genderfluid: describes a person who experiences different genders; their gender can change from day to day or over time

Genderqueer: describes a person whose gender does not conform to the gender binary and/or preconceived ideas of gender; *genderqueer* may be used as either an identity or an umbrella term; some people may use it interchangeably with *nonbinary* and *trans*

Identity: describes who a person is, how they think about themselves, and the other characteristics they use to define themselves

Label: when someone uses a particular word to describe their identity (e.g., *nonbinary, bisexual, queer*, etc.)

Misgender: when someone uses a pronoun or an adjective that does not reflect the gender of the person they're referring to

Nonbinary: describes a person whose gender falls outside the girl-boy binary; *nonbinary* may be used as either an identity or an umbrella term; some people may use it interchangeably with *genderqueer* and *trans*

Pangender: describes a person who is two or more genders (e.g., girl, boy, and/or nonbinary) and typically feels like two or more genders at the same time

Pronouns: how we refer to someone, other than by their name (e.g., she/her/hers, he/him/his, they/them/theirs, xe/xem/xyrs, ze/hir/hirs, ey/em/eirs, etc.); different pronouns can be used in combination as well (e.g., she/they, they/he, they/ey, etc.)

Queer: in reference to gender, describes a person who isn't cisgender; can also be used in reference to sexuality (see below)

Questioning: describes a person in the process of determining their gender; can also be used in reference to sexuality (see below)

Transgender: describes a person who is a gender other than their assigned gender at birth; *transgender* may be used as either an identity or an umbrella term; sometimes shortened to *trans*; some people may use it interchangeably with *nonbinary* and *genderqueer*

Trans man: a man who was assigned female at birth

Trans woman: a woman who was assigned male at birth

Umbrella term: a term that includes other terms or identities (e.g., as an umbrella term, *trans* includes other genders such as nonbinary and bigender; the nonbinary umbrella includes other genders such as agender and demigender)

SEXUALITY & ROMANTIC ATTRACTION

Allosexual: describes a person who experiences attraction to other people

Asexual/aromantic: describes a person who rarely or never experiences attraction to other people; *asexual* and *aromantic* may be used as either identities or umbrella terms

Attraction: the feeling someone experiences when they are drawn to or interested in another person; different types of attraction include sexual, romantic, physical, and emotional

Bisexual/biromantic: describes a person who experiences attraction to people of two or more genders (e.g., girl, boy, and/or nonbinary)

Coming out: describes someone who is not heterosexual voluntarily sharing their sexuality; can also be used in reference to gender (see above)

Demisexual/demiromantic: describes a person who must have an emotional bond before experiencing attraction to another person; falls within the asexual umbrella

Gay: often used to describe a person who experiences attraction to people of their same gender, in particular a man who is attracted to other men; some people may use it as an umbrella term for all queer-related identities

Heterosexual/heteroromantic: describes a woman who only experiences attraction to men, or a man who only experiences attraction to women

Lesbian: generally used to describe a woman who experiences attraction to other women

Pansexual/panromantic: describes a person who

experiences attraction to people of all genders, regardless of gender

Queer: in reference to sexuality, describes a person who isn't heterosexual; can also be used in reference to gender (see above)

Questioning: describes a person in the process of determining their sexual orientation; can also be used in reference to gender (see above)

RESOURCES

The Trevor Project: thetrevorproject.org
PFLAG: pflag.org
The Safe Zone Project: thesafezoneproject.com/resources

ACKNOWLEDGMENTS

Let's talk about the incredible team of people I had helping me work on *Jude Saves the World*. I'm eternally grateful. None of this would be possible without you.

Thank you to Andrea Walker (my former literary agent) for believing in Jude and me. You were so lovely to work with, and I'm forever grateful you took me on as a client. It was great working with you! Thank you to Jennifer Azantian (my current literary agent) at Azantian Literary Agency for supporting us on this unexpected journey. And to both of you for having the trans and nonbinary community's back when it matters.

Thank you to Erin Haggett from Scholastic Canada for loving Jude and showering me with such kindness. For working so hard to make the whole process as comfortable as possible. You're absolutely incredible, and I feel blessed to have our paths cross. I knew I could trust you with my heart and soul.

I also want to thank you, Stella Partheniou Grasso, Diane Kerner, and Maral Maclagan from Scholastic Canada, for being so kind and caring about where my deadname would appear during the contract process. It did not go unnoticed or unappreciated.

Thank you to Emily Seife from Scholastic US for taking a chance on us. It's been an absolute pleasure to work with you.

Thank you to Denise Anderson, Nikole Kritikos, Gui Filippone, and the entire team from Scholastic Canada, and Janell Harris, Maeve Norton, Rachel Feld, and the entire team from Scholastic US for your part in *Jude*'s journey.

Thank you to Ricardo Bessa for the beautiful cover. I love the joy on Jude's face.

Thank you to Megan Manzano, Emily Forney, and Jessica Errera for the opportunity to be inspired by your feedback during the querying process. It helped shape *Jude* into what it is today. Thank you to Blue MacLellan for your kind and wonderful feedback during the early reader process.

Thanks to Ashley Herring Blake, Rebecca Podos, Beth Phelan, and Eric Smith for being inspirational and kind people. I've learned so much from each of you.

Thank you to my mother, Sheila Riley, for being an incredible role model and ally. I couldn't have become the person I am today without your unconditional love and support. To my aunts and uncle and my grandmother for believing in my writing even before you read any of it.

Thank you to my partner, Juliana Johnson, for listening to

me talk about *Jude* nonstop, supporting me, and even going as far as to edit the rough drafts. I owe you one (or a million). I love you and our fur babies (Tilly, Minnie, Sophie, and Charlie) with everything I am. And for the whole Johnson clan cheering me on—thank you for letting me be part of your wonderful and loving family.

A special thank-you to Abbey Owens for always being my cheerleader and for those soul-healing hangouts, Christa Bohan for reading my worst drafts and making me laugh on Bad Days, Rachael Weeks for reminding me that I am an author over and over and believing in me as fiercely as you do, and Erica Miceli for your old-soul friendship. Thank you to Heather McCorquodale, Kelly Lang, and Makela Barnes for always supporting me in a million different ways. Thank you to Grace Dixon, Joanna Allison, and Jeff Bennett for being so kind and encouraging. Thank you to Raiven Grace for always believing in me half a world away. Thank you to my favorite nerd; you know who you are. Thank you to Elijah Abel for keeping me humble. And a special thank-you to Charlotte Dunnell for your support and all the laughter and love you bring into my life.

Thank you to my extended family and cheerleaders (in alphabetical order): A.J. Sass, Andrea O., AM KuarSingh, Aoife Kearney, Ariel Varner, Ash Van Otterloo, Cale

Dietrich, Carter McCormick, Cass Moskowitz, C.B. Lee, Des Rae Smith, Emily Elizabeth Fogle, Esme Symes-Smith, Ezster Mucsi, Finch Kulp, Finch Rimby, Gabi Burton, Kaitlyn Hannah, Kalie Holford, Kelsey Desmond, Logan Trask, M.A. Kendall, Martin Buckingham, Nicole Smith, Peter Dzliums, Reese, S.B., Scout Rodenbaugh, Shelly Page, Terrance Pettitt, and the entire Yellow Gardens gang.

Thank you to my QS friends Caroline Huntoon, Jen St. Jude, Justine Pucella Winans, and Kate Fussner for all your love and support. Happy to be debuting with you! (Go read their wonderful books!)

Thank you to my therapist, Stacey Hatch, for helping me get through a difficult time in my life. *Jude* could not exist without your help, kindness, and feminism. You are incredible at what you do. Thank you for giving me my own safe space.

Thank you to my high school teachers who helped shape me into the person I am today.

Thank you to the librarians, booksellers, and anyone who champions *Jude* in the real world. You're rock stars.

And finally, a thank-you and a shout-out to my writing crews: ATP, RR Bookish, Inkwell, and my Twitter friends. You all are amazing, and I can't wait to see where life and your stories take you.

Without each of you, I would be nothing. Thank you from the very bottom of my heart to the farthest star in the galaxy for always being there for me, for loving me so unconditionally, and supporting me without hesitation. It means *everything*. I love you all dearly.

ABOUT THE AUTHOR

Ronnie Riley (they/them) is a queer, nonbinary, neurodivergent, disabled author living with their partner in Ontario, Canada. They love tea, chocolate, and a cat (or six) nearby while they are writing or reading.

They can be found on Twitter at @mxronnieriley, via email at mxronnieriley.books@gmail.com, or online at mxronnieriley.com.